The Seven Story House

Edited by Simon Easton

This is a work of fiction. Names, characters, businesses, places, events and incidents are either the products of the author's imagination or used in a fictitious manner. Any resemblance to actual persons, living or dead, or actual events is purely coincidental.

WINTERFIELD PRESS

To K. Lynn

Thank you for all your knowledge and support.
Good luck.

Contents

Goldilocks

Samantha Bryant

DEBBIE WALKED ACROSS the field, still wet from the rainstorm she'd been caught in the night before -- the one she spent beneath an underpass trying to huddle in the center where the rain couldn't reach. If her sneakers hadn't already been soaked, walking across the field would have done the job. As it was, she hardly noticed the additional wetness. She was already wet to her knees anyway and cursing herself for her stupidity with every additional step.

A house sat a few hundred yards back from the road. It had that lonely look of an abandoned house and she thought it might do for a night's shelter. She definitely didn't want to walk any further without a chance to dry out her clothes, especially her shoes. It had to be better than another night outside, even if it was technically trespassing.

The sun had nearly disappeared behind the mossy, crumbling chimney by the time she made it to the door, so she took out her flashlight. She held it upright in her hand so it would be useful as a light or a weapon, whichever she found she needed most. She had regretted the weight of the large, heavy flashlight many times in the past few days of traveling by foot, but she found it comforting now.

The door to the house hung ajar. The glass panel beside it lay shattered on the broken-down porch. That boded well for getting in, but less well for what she'd find once inside. Probably a variety of rodents and other field creatures had made their homes in there. From the condition of the clapboard, she guessed it had been at least twenty years since the house had been occupied by anyone who cared for it.

She kicked the door the rest of the way open and stood to the side in case anything large enough to hurt her wanted to rush out. The hinges creaked a horrible metallic shriek, a sound that set her teeth on edge. She waited, flashlight aloft. When nothing menacing announced its presence, Debbie stepped through the doorway gingerly, accompanied by only a few night bugs and a large white-winged moth.

The last rays of fading light shown through the broken panes of the windows and revealed a living room. Whoever abandoned the house must have done so in a hurry -- the living room was still fully furnished, including an enormous and heavy-looking 1970s era television set with a pair of honest-to-God rabbit ears. A crumpled bit of tin foil rested over the base, collecting dust. Debbie took in the heavy floral furnishings and cheesy pictures of the Precious Moments praying girl dangling crookedly over the sofa and laughed. Someone's grandmother had suffered from a home shopping network addiction. "Hi Grandma," she called to the room with a bravado she didn't really feel. "Got anything to eat?"

Hearing no answer, Debbie stepped to the nearest armchair and kicked it with her squishy-wet sneaker, raising a cloud of dust and releasing a musty smell into the already stale and stagnant air of the room. Several alarmingly large and many-legged bugs scuttled up the arms and into the cushions. She wouldn't be making her bed on any of this furniture tonight. She'd prefer to sleep alone, thank you.

She clicked on her flashlight and turned to examine the rest of what could be seen by its light, hoping to find somewhere to rest. The living room made up most of the bottom floor of the house. One wall was a large fireplace. Debbie knelt and shined her light up the chimney. She heard scurrying sounds and hurried to get a fire lit before any furry friends could get too close. She had matches and a lighter in her backpack, and there were some old newspapers and magazines spilled on the floor, so she felt sure she could get a fire started. She'd burn pieces of the house itself if she had to so she could be dry and warm.

She shivered in spite of the warm summer air and hoped she wasn't going to get sick. It had been stupid of her, sleeping beneath the underpass. Stubborn and stupid. Sure, she'd been tired and hadn't wanted to keep walking, but she hadn't rested well and it definitely hadn't been worth the day's walk in waterlogged sneakers. She should have kept walking until she found something better. It was just another in the string of bad decisions that brought her to this point. Now, she was going to have blisters and catch a cold, and there were still a lot of miles between here and home. She'd always had a hard time finding the right path and staying on it.

At last the fire took and the newspapers and magazines crumpled as they were consumed. By firelight, she spotted a small wooden chair sitting by the wall. When she picked it up, it fell into pieces. Just right, she thought to herself, and lugged the fragments to the fireplace and tossed them in.

The fire blazed after that, and Debbie sat to remove her wet shoes and pants. Her skin was clammy and cold. She spread the clothes out on the hearthstone, watching carefully to be sure that the flames were staying contained and the smoke was actually going up the chimney. The crackling and popping sounds were comforting, like the voices of old friends. She dug through her backpack again, pushing aside her notebook and bag of soiled clothes, and pulling out a pair of mostly dry socks and some shorts and finding a tin of canned meat. It wasn't enough to eat, but it was the end of what she'd brought with her, so it would have to do, even if she was still hungry.

Sitting as near the fire as she dared, she turned her body to heat one side then the other, lifting her long, blonde hair to better feel the heat on her back and arms. She smelled terrible. She'd have to find a way to bathe before letting her brother see her. She didn't want him to know how bad she had let things get.

Listening to the wind blowing through the trees, she relaxed a bit. It was peaceful here in the house in the woods. She had always found comfort in small, homey sounds like rustling leaves and crackling fires. If the house was cleaner, she might have stayed here a good, long while. She hadn't told anyone she was coming, so it wasn't like she was expected at a certain time. She could do this at her own pace.

She picked up a sneaker and tried to wring it out, but it was no good. They would take hours to dry out and that meant she'd be here for the night.

She sat and watched the fire blaze. It grew large enough that she had to move further away from it. Her stomach rumbled and she wished she'd gone ahead and spent her last ten dollars on a full breakfast this morning instead of settling for the oatmeal just because it was cheap. The ten dollars wouldn't make the rest of her journey easier. It wasn't enough to buy a ride or a bed. She leaned over and rummaged through the pocket of her drying jeans, pulled the bill out, and smoothed it against her thigh, studying it in the unsteady light of the fire. It was her last money in this world. And it wasn't even really hers.

She'd stolen it, along with the rest of fifty-odd dollars, from Steven four days earlier when she'd finally left. The little backpack with her few clothes, a few cans of food, the flashlight, and her notebook had been all she'd taken -- less than she had arrived with when she came to Richmond.

It wasn't that far from Steven's place in Richmond to her hometown of Hillsborough, North Carolina. At least that's what she'd told herself when she'd started. But there's a big difference in distance measured by miles on a bus and miles on your own two feet. Now exhausted and faced with another fifty or sixty miles to go, she was beginning to doubt she could make it. Stubbornness could only take you so far.

She had felt that going home was something she needed to do under her own power. Walking had seemed like a way she could lay claim to the experience, to declare her independence. She would get there on her own, without taking help from anybody. She'd had enough of the kind of help the world had offered her anyway, these past few months.

It had started out well enough, her life in Richmond. She'd left home when her mother died. Without Mama Bear, she'd felt unmoored and trapped at the same time. On little more than a whim, she decided she had to strike out on her own right then or she'd be trapped forever.

She'd packed up her notebook and clothes and spent all her graduation money on a bus ticket to Richmond. She'd been there before and thought it was nice. She knew a few people she could crash with until she got on her feet. It had been okay. She'd waited tables and run the cash register at a gas station. It hadn't been easy, but she was getting by.

If Steven hadn't crossed her path like some kind of black cat and changed her luck and her life, she might have continued like that for years. He called her Goldie, fondling the strands of her hair with his thick grease-stained fingers. No one had ever given her a pet name before, not even her parents, and she had liked it. She had liked the mischief in his smile, too, and the strength in his hands, until he took to using both against her.

He apologized, of course, and promised it wouldn't happen again, but she knew better. His words were only words. She'd seen his kind before: the man with an animal inside. Her father had been such a man. Her mother had protected her, but she'd seen the bruises he'd left, on her skin and on her soul. She'd be damned if she'd let anyone do that to her. So, she'd left. Debbie didn't need any more bears or wolves. The next man in her life, she decided, if there ever was one, would be a dog.

4

Something, soft and warm and loyal. A friend.

Ironically, the only place she really had to go was back home-- she'd used up all her favors and burned too many bridges in her months with Steven. So, it was back to the very place she'd run from. Back to her father.

Of course, her father was a toothless bear these days. He probably wouldn't know who she was, let alone try to enact any kind of punishment on her for running away. Her brother Griffin said the old man didn't remember much of anyone anymore though sometimes he tried to pretend that he did. Maybe that was good. Maybe they could have a fresh start, meeting as strangers. Maybe she could forget their past, too.

After all, it was better to dream about where you were going than stand around regretting where you'd been. Hillsborough, she guessed, was both of those -- where she was going and where she had been, her dream and her regret all rolled into one.

Debbie stood and stretched. She didn't like the paths her mind had wandered down. It was too hot there by the fire now that the pieces of the chair had really caught. It was time for a distraction. She checked, but her clothes were still too wet. Sock feet would have to do. Debbie decided to explore the upstairs rooms of Grandma's house in the wood and see if she could find a place to rest or anything she could use to improve her lot for the rest of the journey. Treasure hunt, she thought.

When she and her brother Griffin were kids, they had spent a lot of time exploring their grandmother's house. The big, rambling home had a lot of unused rooms that had once belonged to their aunts and uncles. They had found amazing things in there -- a chest full of trophies, closets full of clothes, ribbons, books and maps, and, once, even a gun. They'd both been afraid to touch it, but had stood still, staring at it for what felt like hours. It was gone the next time they visited.

Exploring wouldn't be the same without a playmate, but Debbie was curious about this house she had ended up in. Who knew what she might find upstairs? Standing at the bottom of the stairs, Debbie leaned forward, trying to see what awaited her. She couldn't see much. It was dark up there.

Debbie looked up the stairwell doubtfully, wondering if it would support her weight. "One way to find out, I suppose," she muttered, then placed one foot on the bottom stair. It held. She worked her way up the stairwell, one stair at a time, testing each step for sureness before committing her full weight. One step at a time, she arrived at the top of the stairwell.

A long narrow hall stretched ahead, with doors leading off to the sides, two on each side. She shined her flashlight along the floor and didn't see any scurrying mice or insects. She realized she could actually see pretty well, better than she could see downstairs. The moon all but filled the long window at the end of the hall and cast the hallway in a white, pale light.

Debbie opened the first door. She felt something was amiss, but she couldn't figure out what it was. A large bed took up the center of the room, and a matching dresser rested against the wall. The room looked nice enough though it smelled rotten; it had probably been the master bedroom. Then she realized she was looking out at the sky, not through a window, but through a massive hole in the roof. She took another step forward, then hurriedly backed out of the room. The floor had sagged beneath her foot. It was probably rotten through. She had no intention of dying for a game of Treasure Hunt. A breeze came up from somewhere and she shivered. She turned around. "Too cold," she said.

The door directly across the hall was already open. She stepped into the doorway and shined her light around. This room looked intact so she stepped inside. The walls were strangely reflective and glossy and she slowly realized they were wet, water running down them in slow, steady rivulets. The rain had stopped in the early afternoon. There was no reason for the walls to still be dripping and Debbie felt a sick sort of undefined dread.

An old crib squatted in the middle of the room like a forgotten animal trap. The sight of it made her feel strange. It didn't help when a wind blew through the hole in the ceiling across the hall and the crib rocked a little with a creaking sound. "Too creepy," she said and backed into the hall, bumping into a small table she hadn't noticed against the wall. The dusty knick-knacks on top clattered, the sound loud in the quiet house.

Next door to the nursery was a bathroom, which stunk of something rancid or dead like a mouse had died in the walls. That left one last door to open.

Debbie stood outside the door, digging her toes into the pile of the carpet as if she could anchor herself that way. She had the oddest feeling that she should knock. She raised her hand to do so, but when she bumped the door with her knuckle, it creaked open.

A beautiful little girl's bedroom was revealed, just the kind of room Debbie had coveted as a child. A canopy bed was near the window, and a round braided rug on the floor. Debbie couldn't help herself. She walked in and shined her light around to explore. The room was perfect, other than the dust. The walls and windows were sound; water had not leaked through the ceiling. The bed was even made.

Debbie wondered if she dared rest there. It looked so perfect and inviting and she was so tired. She picked up a doll off a nearby shelf and tossed it onto the bed. Nothing happened. She had half-expected a mouse or some other furry critter to run off. Goading herself to be brave, she grabbed the comforter by one corner and flung it back. She shined her light all around and found only a spider, which she flicked off the bed unceremoniously. She touched the mattress, pushing down to make the bed bounce and heard nothing but mildly squeaky bedsprings.

Maybe it would be okay to lie down, just for a few hours. She was exhausted. She climbed into the bed and turned off the flashlight, cradling it like a teddy bear in her arms. "Just right," she murmured as she fell asleep.

❧

She didn't know how long she had been asleep when she woke, or what had wakened her. But her heart was racing and she felt very alert. She sat up in the bed, pulling the covers up as if they might afford some protection from whatever danger she faced. There at the foot of the bed were three people--a family, she guessed: mother, father, and child.

"What are you doing here, girl?" the man asked, his voice low, but not angry. He sounded more wary than threatening. Still, Debbie's heart raced.

"I thought it was abandoned," she said.

"This was my mother's house," said the woman. She sounded like she might cry. She gripped her husband's arm and he pushed her part way behind him like he thought Debbie might be some kind of danger to her.

"I didn't mean --"

"Who are you?" the boy asked. "What are you doing in that bed?"

Debbie disentangled her limbs from the blankets and scrambled out of the bed, clutching her flashlight in both hands like a baseball bat.

"I just needed a place to rest and get dry. I didn't know --"

The family turned towards her and Debbie backed to the door. "I'll just go," she said and turned and fled down the stairs. She moved so fast that her sock-clad feet slipped on the wooden stairs and she nearly toppled down them, but she found her footing and hurried back to the fireplace. She pulled her stiff jeans on over her shorts and shoved her feet into the shoes, keeping one eye on the stairs for the first sign of the family coming after her. She thought she could hear the adults arguing. She wasn't going to stick around to find out what they decided to do about her trespassing.

Hoisting the backpack onto her shoulder, she hurried towards the door and tugged it open. Soft light from the approaching dawn lit the porch and the field beyond. Debbie dared a look back and found the child, a boy with large, solemn eyes, standing at the foot of the stairs watching her. She smiled and waved as she stepped through the doorway and he raised a hand in return. It must have been a trick of the light that it looked more like a paw. Debbie ran back toward the road promising herself that she'd stick to the path until it took her home.

About The Author

Samantha Bryant believes in love, magic, and unexplainable connections between people. Her favorite things are lonely beaches, untamed cliff tops, sunlight through the leaves of trees, summer rains, and children's laughter. She has lived in many places, including rural Alaska, Kansas, Kentucky, Vermont, England and Spain. She is fierce at heart though she doesn't look it.

She's a fan of Charlotte Brontë, William Shakespeare, Emily Dickinson, Neil Gaiman, Nicole Perlman, and Joss Whedon, among many others. She would like to be Amy Tan when she grows up, but so far it doesn't look like she'll be growing up anytime soon.

Samantha writes blogs, poems, essays, and novels. You can buy her debut novel Going Through the Change: A Menopausal Superhero Novel on Amazon, or ask them to order it at your favorite bookstore. Mostly she writes about things that scare or worry her. It's cheaper than therapy. Someday, she hopes to make her living solely as a writer. In the meantime, she also teaches middle school Spanish, which, admittedly, is an odd choice for money-earning, especially in North Carolina. When she's not writing or teaching, Samantha enjoys time with her family, watching old movies, baking, reading, and going places. Her favorite gift is tickets (to just about anything).

Steel Will

Sarah Sugg

H i honey, what's wrong?" I asked, immediately puzzled and worried. My husband never called that early.

"Meredith, look on the kitchen counter. I think I left my cell phone this morning."

"Yeah, I see it. It's still plugged in."

"Will you bring it to me?" he asked? "We'll have lunch in Georgetown at that French restaurant you like."

"No, even crepes at Bonaparte's won't make me drive in all that traffic. You come home or live a day without your cell phone," I said, never considering for a minute driving into DC. We live in Old Town Alexandria in an ancient yellow colonial. I could have walked down King Street and caught the Metro, but the Metro had never caught on with me. It still scared me.

"Well, if I can get time, I'll come get it. If it rings, just let it go to voicemail. I'm not expecting anything important. Why don't you just cut it off?" he said, sounding weird.

"Sure, no problem. Anything else?" I asked, looking at his cell phone. It wasn't like mine. I always got his reject phones. I didn't even know how to cut it off for sure. I didn't let him know how clueless I was.

"No, see you tonight if not sooner."

It was like he wanted me to check his texts. He wasn't password protected and he's a password fanatic. The first thing I did was to read the texts between him and his girlfriend, Betsy. I realized that some of them were before my miscarriage. The next thing was to go to the bank and take $30,000 out of our joint savings account and open my own account at the bank down the street. I didn't touch the investments.

Then I went to the local pawn shop and pawned my expensive

wedding rings. I was given $2,000 for them. I know Paul paid much more, but they were trash to me, and $2,000 was okay.

I think I was mad for the first time in my life.

Paul and I had been married for seven years. We had a lovely home, good jobs, and a sound, loving marriage. At least that was what I thought. I should have been crushed, but I was mainly mad.

I drove my little Toyota that was in Paul's name -- everything was in his name -- to a used car dealer and bought a Kia Sedona van. I paid for it with our joint checking account. The check would bounce, but the overdraft protection would cover it. I would need all the money in my new account to pay for my new life. He could sell the Toyota to get his money back. The dealer helped with insurance and plates. I told them I would take a taxi and pick up the van when they opened at seven thirty the next day. All this was done with a steel will I didn't even know I had. I was furious, but for some reason it felt good.

It was late afternoon when I walked in the door. Paul was sitting in the living room with a scotch texting on his cell phone. Who to? I wondered. Who had a mistress named Betsy? Sonya or Maya, maybe, but Betsy sounded so wholesome.

"Hi, babe, where have you been? I tried calling you on your cell phone. Is it cut off for some reason?" he asked quickly, looking up at me.

"I don't know. I'll check it later."

"Want to go out for supper? I need to meet someone around nine, but we should be through eating and home by then," he said, sipping his drink.

"Let's go to that new seafood restaurant near the water and eat outside under the stars," I said, knowing Mr. Cheap would balk at that.

"That's a little expensive isn't it? This is just supper. I thought maybe Italian," he said, as he finished off his scotch and smiled a big executive smile at me. How I ever trusted him, I'll never know. While he still looked good at thirty-five, he so obviously leaked slime. Before that day, I had totally believed in him. I was so naive.

"Oh, baby, let's make it a special night," I said, slipping the van papers in the kitchen drawer. "We can eat out under the stars, drink expensive champagne, have steak and lobster then you can go to your meeting. I'll take a long hot bubble bath and be waiting for you in bed when you get back. Maybe we'll make that baby tonight. I'm ovulating," I crooned with a coy smile.

"Maybe we could make it now?" he said, never being one to miss a poke.

"Okay, but you'll be late for your meeting because I'm not giving up food," I said with a big fake smile. We had been trying to make a baby for months now and nothing happened. I had been pregnant in November but lost my baby boy at five months. I wanted a child. I was still married, so I thought I would give it one more try. Besides, it might be years before I would get another chance to sleep with a man. I was going to a rural area where the pick of men was slim to drunk and unemployed.

"We can eat fast or you can get take out. Let's go make this baby," he said, giving me one of his big grins. The grin had not made it to his wary eyes.

I went into the bathroom and looked at myself in the mirror. I could do this, I thought as I sprayed the very expensive potent perfume he liked in my long red hair. No one in my family had this wiry red hair. My blond mom would say God gave it to me when I asked where it came from. With this perfume all over me, Paul would smell like an expensive whore when he went to his "meeting."

Paul was naked and waiting for me in our king sized bed. He worked out and, like everything in his life, he did a good job. He was trim and except for his hair thinning out on top, he looked good. I let him undress me like he enjoys doing. Like I was a new conquest, I guess. I did all the special things he liked. I wanted him to remember what he was missing when he got home tomorrow night. Because tomorrow night, I would be gone. I pretended I was asleep when he left for his meeting. He had kissed me on my hip before he slipped out of the apartment smelling like very strong men's cologne. He had tried to cover my perfume.

When I was sure he was gone, I congratulated myself for living through the sex and pulled out our expensive suitcases and dumped all my drawers into them. One suitcase just held shoes. I had to leave my hanging clothes and jewelry box out because he might notice they were missing when he got home. I'd get them in the morning. I went into the attic and got down my Christmas ornaments that had belonged to both my grandmothers and my mother. I took the artificial tree too. Paul didn't need it. They were all hidden in the guest room closet. The last box I got out of the attic was marked Baby and held all the things I bought before my miscarriage last year. I walked around the house quietly, mentally marking what was mine. I would pack it up in the morning when I got the van.

Wearily I got back in bed and waited for Paul. Doubt started flooding my mind. I was thirty-two and until now had done very little on my own. This house was only a block away from where I grew up. Until my mother died seven years ago, my life had pretty much been the same. Until today, I'd been perfectly content. In fact, most of my life I had been loved and satisfied with life. I could have pretended I didn't read his texts and life would have continued as it was. Being on my own would be uncharted territory, and I was beginning to lose my will.

I planned to seduce him one more time when he got home. He's so easy. For some reason, the fact that he had probably been with someone else was a little turn on. Could he perform again so soon? Did he use safe sex with her?

When his alarm went off, I woke out of a deep dreamless sleep. Somehow he sneaked back without waking me up. Morning sex had never been my favorite, but I needed as much sperm as I could get to make this baby before I left. Despite my earlier doubts, I decided to leave the minute I woke up.

"Good morning, baby maker. How about one more time? I'll do all the work. You can just lay there and pretend you're dead," I crooned. That was one of his favorite scenarios.

"What's got into you? Well, who cares? This is nice," he said, jumping up to use the bathroom.

He was late getting to work. This drives him crazy because he says ten minutes makes thirty minutes worth of traffic delay. "My whole day is ruined," he griped as he got ready. The afterglow from sex had long since passed for him.

It wasn't as ruined as it was going to be by the end of the day. He was going to be so mad when he discovered I was gone.

I do contract work for local museums when they have major events like a showing of the Queen's jewels. Currently, I had nothing going on. It's usually feast or famine, but lucrative for part-time work. As soon as he left, I quickly washed up and put on some jeans and a green William and Mary sweatshirt, and called a taxi to go pick up my van. I wanted to be on the road for Henderson by noon, and I still had to pack the van.

My grandmother had left me her house and thirty acres of land in the countryside near Henderson. She died just before Paul and I married. I went down alone to the funeral and all I had done since was hired someone to cut the grass and paid the taxes. What was I going to find? I had a tent and planned to pitch it in the house if need be. I had my gun and knew how to use it. I didn't know what to expect, but I could handle it.

I got off of US-1 and turned on to Warrenton Road. I only had a few more miles to go.

I had loved being married to Paul. The weekend before, we had talked about how lucky we were to be so happy. He must have gotten a kick out of that. I had loved how proud he was to be seen with me. He had bought most of my clothes and all my lingerie since we'd been married because his taste was better than mine. I knew he was proud of my jobs with the museums. I'd heard him brag to his friends many times. He wasn't as devastated about the miscarriage as I was, but he was supportive. If I hadn't seen those texts and emails on his phone, I would be happy and looking forward to our planned weekend with his mother at Cape May.

A little voice in my head that sounded a lot like my grandmother whispered, "Child, Paul has never left his phone before. He did it on purpose, hoping you would snoop and do exactly what you did. You need to figure out why."

"I bet the sex confused him or, more probably, he saw through my last desperate tries to have his baby and was still laughing," I replied out loud to the voice in my head. Needless to say, the cracks in my steel were sealed up and I was angry enough to start on my new adventure.

ॐ∘ॐ

I pulled into the yard and was greeted by daffodils next to an old rundown house that desperately needed love and painting. Several dogwoods were ready to bloom. You could see where crocus had already bloomed next to the droopy steps. There were bluebirds fussing at me for being close to their nest in the eaves of the porch. It was like they were saying "Go away, go away. It's our house now."

My steel will was stronger than ever. The rusted tin roof had come unattached in one place and you could see into the attic. My first call would be to a roofer because the roof was in sad shape. I thought a nice blue metal roof would be nice.

The porch was in fairly good shape. I looked up and you could see the ceiling was still a faded sky blue, haunt blue. The floor was a chipped gray. I remembered sitting in a rocking chair and staring at that ceiling and wishing I had visited my grandmother more often. Her graveside funeral was the first time I'd ever been to the house. She had always traveled to us.

I had the key to the front door. The door opened surprisingly easily. Sheets covered the furniture and the refrigerator door was open. It had been emptied by some kind stranger. The beds were made with dust covers. Mice droppings were everywhere, and here and there was significant water damage probably, from the roof. Upstairs the blinds were falling down and slats were hanging every which way. I just yanked them down and threw them down the stairs. I was tired and hungry so I drove into Henderson and ate at McDonald's. Paul hated fast food. I used the bathroom before I left hoping that the trip would last me until I came back for breakfast. I planned to eventually pitch a tent in the house until it was livable.

If it had been any other house, I would have walked away from it. Instead, I grabbed my old green sleeping bag and got comfortable in the front seat. I couldn't lean back because of all the boxes, but I was so tired it didn't matter. My mind went back to the pawn shop ticket I left for Paul. I left it on the kitchen table with a note saying Betsy might enjoy the rings if he got them back. That's all I said. Not where I was, nor did I say "Rot in hell, scum." I was a lady.

"Just like he probably hoped you would be," the voice in my head said.

The morning sun woke me up. I had to go to the bathroom in the worst way and wasn't sure when McDonald's opened. I unlocked the door to the cold house and sprinted to the cold, nasty toilet. I had just sat down when there was a pounding on the front door.

"Sheriff's Office, open up!"

I jumped up as soon as I could and ran out pulling my pants up as I went. I was just zipping them up when I opened the door.

"Yes," I said, peering around the door at the serious looking deputy in front of me.

"Who else you got in there?" he said, looking at me zipping my jeans.

"Nobody, you caught me peeing," I responded. "This is my house. I'm going to move in today as soon as I get rid of the mouse poop. Do you need to see paperwork or something?"

"What's your name?" he asked, looking into my eyes to see if I was lying or drugged, I guess.

"Meredith Winstead Smith-Hein, sir," I said. "My driver's license is in the car. I'll go get it if you need it."

"Yeah, why don't you do that. Plan to stay long?" he asked.

"I plan to stay forever. I may go back and forth to D.C. for work, but from now on this is my base. I'm home." It felt like I was home and it felt good.

"Okay. Sounds like a plan. By North Carolina law, you can't stay in a house without electricity and running water. You'll need to get your utilities turned on in Henderson today," he said, scanning my driver's license into something he had on his phone. "I drive by here on the way to work every day so I'll be checking."

"I'll go after I eat breakfast," I said, noticing I had mouse poop on my white shirt.

"Say, would you be interested in some cats? My mother has eight kittens we can let you have right now," the officer said looking at the poop smear on my shirt.

"One or two kittens, but I must have a big cat. Kittens don't chase mice and I have a lot of mice."

"I'll see what I can do. Keep your doors locked. This is the country and it's not as safe as it used to be. If I can, I'll get the cats out to you this afternoon after I get off. Bob Kincaid is my name, by the way."

I shut the door and walked around the house trying to decide what to do first. Trinkets were still on the dusty shelves; my grandmother's clothes were still on the hangers in her closet. Her mended white cotton gown that she wore every night hung sadly on a poof satin hanger just as she left it on her last day. I smelled it, but her scent was long gone. Strangely, nothing had been touched or vandalized since she died. I cried a little as I touched her things. Suddenly there was pounding on the door again.

"Sheriff's Office," Kincaid shouted. I rushed to answer the door.

"Your husband has reported you missing. In the report he states you have been distraught since a miscarriage several months ago."

"I found texts from his mistress dating back to when I was in the hospital bleeding away my baby. That just hurt. I bet he was sitting in my hospital room texting her. He's had her for a while," I said, losing my will of steel for a few seconds. "They say a woman knows when her husband is cheating, but until I looked at his texts and email, I was clueless."

"I'm sorry, ma'am. I have to let the authorities know we found you, and that you want to stay missing as far as he's concerned."

Officer Kincaid looked thoughtful for a moment.

"You know, you look familiar. Are you related to the old lady who used to live here?"

"She was my grandmother," I said, giving him a proud smile.

"Where did you get that red hair? From your dad?" he asked, looking at me funny.

"I had a wonderful stepfather but never knew my dad. My mom used to say God gave me this red hair. Both my grandmother and my mother had fine blond hair. This hair, it's a blessing and a curse sometimes. I guess now I can cut some of it off. My husband liked it long."

"My wife, Lena, and I have four girls. They all have red hair. One has hair just like yours. You must be kin somewhere down the line. Listen, I'll go now. Don't forget to get your lights and water turned on. What are you going to do about that roof?"

"I plan to go to Henderson today and also call some roofing people."

"Here's my card. I'll write my home number on it. Call my wife, Lena, if you have any questions about the area. We thought a lot of your grandmother. My wife's mother did her cleaning. We'd love to have you come to church with us."

"Thanks. I'll go into town this morning and sleep in the car another night if it doesn't work out," I told him with my hands on hips. "I plan to pitch a tent inside the house until the varmint problem is under control anyway."

"That tent isn't such a bad idea," he said, laughing as he got in his cruiser.

⁂

I couldn't get the lights cut on until there was an inspection because the house hadn't been lived in for more than two years. It could be days before the inspector could get to me. The water was on. All I had to do was cut it on in front of the house. This part of the county got water years ago. I had to pay for the hook up even when I didn't live in the house. It was a blessing now.

I spent my time sweeping up mouse poop and unpacking. The roofer would be here on Monday and thought he could finish in two days.

I worked on the kitchen all day. I boiled water on my camp stove and washed every dish in the kitchen. I wiped mountains of poop out of the cupboards and scrubbed with pure Clorox. My William and Mary sweatshirt was ruined and I had had it from my college days. With the boxes and small bits of furniture I packed in the van inside the house, I was able to put my twin-sized air mattress in the back and slept fine.

Anxiously, I waited on the inspector. He came late the next day and said I needed the house rewired. Mice had been chewing on the old wires and the house was dangerous. After he left, I just cried. I'm not sure why I cried, but the minute he left, I lost it. This is how Bob Kincaid's poor brother found me.

"Man! Is this a bad time? My brother told me to bring you these cats. He's busy with a double homicide or something. My name is Eric Kincaid. This big cat here is mine," he said, walking through the door I left open for light. He nervously ignored the fact that I was on the floor crying. "He is one of the best mousers there is. I want him back, but you can keep him for a couple of weeks."

I sat up and swiped my face with the mouse poop rag I was holding. I know he saw it because he made a yuck face. He stood in the door trying to hold a big male alley cat who was not in a good mood. He was good looking in his scuffed cowboy boots and a not-so-clean white t-shirt.

"I'll go get the kittens and my mother's wild barn cat. She is a female so unless you want a lot of cats, you need to get her fixed soon. My mom says she'll tame easy enough."

While he was getting the other cats, I stood up and washed my face in the kitchen sink. The cold slightly rusty water felt good. I looked at the big cat and he looked at me as if to say, let's get on with it. I quickly opened all the cabinets so he could do his job. You could tell he was used to being the boss.

"Here are the kittens. I would keep them in another room for awhile. Old Tom here isn't used to babies," he said. "I let the other cat loose in the back. Feed her on the porch until she's tame. Her mother was a house cat so she should tame up," he said, looking at the door as if wanting to escape. "My mom sent some cat food."

"Thanks, sorry about how I was when you came. I just found out

I have to have this house rewired before the city will turn the lights on. Do you know any electricians?"

"This is your and my lucky day, sweet lady. I just got back from Wilson where I helped wire a huge new office building. It took six weeks. I'll be glad to wire this house for you."

"Wonderful. Look around and give me an estimate. I'll need to see your license, but it sounds great to me. Want a Coke? I have some in a cooler."

❧❦

Eric and I worked side-by-side for three days because he said he would give me a cost break if I would help. He even did the wall mending when he finished.

Most of the rooms had beadboard that had been painted many times. The water didn't damage the walls terribly due to all that paint. I still needed to repaint the whole house. He restrung a wire to the barn so I would have light in an old workshop and also put searchlights on the barn that lit up the whole yard. He did all this for $2,000.

I paid him with a check from my new bank account and thanked him. We celebrated with pizza and beer when the inspection passed and the lights came on. That's how Paul found us, half drunk, sitting on the floor around a pizza box, laughing and eating pizza.

"This is your husband?" Eric said, slowly getting up. You could tell he had been in this situation more than once and half of him thought it was funny and the other half was concerned. "Here's my card. Call me if you have any problems," he said, leaving out the front door. I could hear his loud truck start and rumble down the road.

"Who's your friend?" Paul said through clenched teeth.

"My electrician, and I think he's a cousin way down the line. He's been very helpful. How did you find me and why are you here?"

"This house was on our taxes every year. It wasn't hard. I wanted to talk to you. Meredith, you know I've always had girlfriends the entire time we've been married, and I've still kept you happy. Some men need more than one woman can give."

"How would I know you were cheating? Did Betsy call me or did I find lipstick on your collar? I didn't look because I trusted you," I said, thinking what an idiot I had been.

"Come on home, be my wife, and let's pretend nothing happened.

You loved your life. My family loves you. Hell, even my boss loves you."

"All you care about is yourself. Your mother is the only one I'll miss."

"Just the other day you were saying how good our marriage was," he said in that voice I usually gave into.

"That's before I knew about Betsy. I trusted you and you're right, I loved our marriage right up to when I found those texts. It's over now. I'm over you and I don't care if I never see you again. I don't want anything else from you," I said with my steel calm. Strangely I meant every word without an ounce of doubt.

I heard a little voice whisper in my ear, "Don't waiver, you're right."

"What was all that sex about before you left? I bet you wanted a baby so you could get child support and the Hein's inheritance. Well, that's not going to happen. I got a vasectomy after your miscarriage. I didn't like what pregnancy did to your beautiful body," Paul said with a sneer on his face.

I felt like I'd been hit with a brick. I couldn't talk for a while.

The little voice in my head said, "He's lying, he's afraid of the knife." Paul had to be gassed to have dental work done. The voice was right.

"I think you're lying. Please just leave. It only matters if I'm pregnant and it's too early to tell. Now get out of my house or I will call the police."

"You mean our house, half is mine," he said with a sneer.

"No, I came into the marriage with this house. But the house in Alexandria is half mine. Don't forget that. You'll need to sell it or buy me out. Now, please get out."

He left without another word, which was a surprise. He loves to argue and usually got his way.

I went into the living room and sank down into the new rust colored recliner I'd just purchased from Sears. Eric slowly walked in from the kitchen.

"Man, he's a piece of work," he said with a slow sexy smile. I never heard him come in the house or his loud truck drive up.

He knelt down and gave me the sweetest kiss and started massaging my feet. Maybe Paul wasn't the best at everything. Eric comforted me all night. Occasionally it flitted across my totally satisfied brain that he may be my cousin, but surely a second cousin and that's okay in the South.

Eric started spending a lot of time at the house with me. We slept on a mattress in the tent I pitched in the living room. Quickly we got the house in order. The roof man came and put up a nice blue tin roof. After a couple of weeks, the house perked along like it had never been abandoned. It was sad to finally take the tent down. It was like an extra layer of protection from Paul, the world, and the mice.

I put containers of plants and flowers on the porches and even had two goats who mowed the grass for me. Eric said he'd always wanted to do that. I started milking the nanny and planned to make goat cheese soon. In the meantime, I fed the milk to the cats and local critters. I got around three eggs a day from the chickens that just showed up one day. The cats gave them a time, but after a few pecks they left them alone. They may have been feral chickens.

The kittens gave me much joy. Most nights they slept right between Eric and me. Tom slept at the foot of the bed, and barn cat still slept outdoors. She did honor me with a visit inside every day for an hour or so.

Life was good for two months until Eric got a job in Raleigh that would take several months to complete. If they got off early, he drove the hour trip and came home, but most of the week he worked late and stayed in his camper near the job site. Weekends were mine.

Some evenings we went over to see his brother and had supper with the family. His brother had two sets of twin girls and all four had different shades of red hair. Mandy Sue's hair was the same dark carrot red as mine and just as wiry. Her mother put it in a ponytail and it flew behind her like Superman's cape. Her twin had a lighter color red that was soft and beautiful. It was cut in a bob and hung straight around her face. Both the younger twins had soft red curls. One day, Mandy Sue showed me a picture of her grandmother who she said gave her the red hair. She looked enough like me to be me. I took it to her mother.

"Who is this? Could I be related to her?" I asked Lena, Mandy Sue's mother.

"That's Mrs. Kincaid. This boy is Eric and Bob's father. Eric's dad remarried someone younger when his first wife died, and had a whole new family when he was in his sixties."

"Wow, babies at sixty."

"They had Eric, Bob and a sister named Rebecca. She has the

flaming wiry red hair also. She lives in Vermont, as far away from her father as possible, but comes home for Christmas. You look a lot like her also. We've been talking about it since you and Eric hooked up. Speaking of that, I want to warn you that I love Eric to death, but he tends to be a rolling stone if you know what I mean."

"I know, but he's what I need right now. I don't want either of us hurt, though. Do you think we could be related?"

"What's your story? I know you are related to Mrs. Winstead and as far as I know she wasn't related to the Kincaid's. What about your grandfather? Could he be a cousin or something?" she asked.

"I never knew my grandfather. He died before I was born. My grandmother only said good things about him, and I got the feeling he was from up north. He didn't have any family that I'm aware of."

"Your mother moved to Alexandria after college, married your father and had you. Mrs. Winstead would go visit her twice a year on the bus, and loved to tell my mother about her trips. She was so proud of you. My mother kept house for your grandmother for years," Lena said, looking interested in my life.

"I always thought they were wonderful. I've never met my father. My step-father had always been there as long as I can remember. I've never known who my father was," I said, beginning to feel embarrassed. I truly never thought much about fathers or grandfathers. Our family was just fine as it was.

"So you could be related to the Kincaid's through him. Do you have siblings?" Lena asked.

"No, my mother couldn't have any more children after me. She would say I was all she needed. We had a good life together. My whole life until now has been good. I had a wonderful life with my husband until I found out he was cheating. I had a miscarriage five months ago and now I'm afraid I'll have problems like my mother."

"What was her problem?" Lena asked as she wiped down the counter.

"Her uterus was tipped. Nowadays she could have had IVF and had a flock of children. She was a good mother." I said, remembering how beautiful she was. "She died of breast cancer eight years ago. My stepfather grieved himself to death and died of a heart attack soon after. My grandmother died about six months later."

"I'm so sorry. All that loss so close together must have been hard for you."

"I had Paul. He was so good to me through it all. He held me when I cried and did little things to make me feel better. That's why it is so hard to believe he was cheating on me the entire time we were married."

"I don't understand some men," Lena said.

"I certainly don't," I whispered sadly.

"Well for Kincaid family history you need to go see Mr. Kincaid. If you get him on a good day, he can tell you what he had to eat for supper fifty years ago, on a bad day he can't remember his children's names. He had six so it's harder than most. The older ones are in their sixties now. I'm going to see him tomorrow if you want to go with me. We all have a schedule, so someone sees him every day. It keeps the home on their toes and gives them a small break. Oh, by the way, he's not a nice man. He's grabbed me on more than one occasion. Just stay away from the hands."

For some reason, I didn't tell Eric I was meeting Lena and going out to see Mr. Kincaid. I was so worried that we were related and it would mess us up. I waited until he packed up his clean clothes for the week and the food I had prepared and scooted out the door, late as usual. It takes an hour to get to Raleigh with traffic, and he only had forty-five minutes. He wasn't focused like Paul would have been, and that was one of the few things I didn't like about him. I did adore his loving and that was why he was late this time. I now know Paul's love making was choreographed like a ballet and while usually good for me lacked the passion and spontaneity of Eric's all-over-the-place love. I knew he was making love to me and not some waltz in his head.

The phone rang as I was pouring out cat food. Almost no one calls me anymore. It was Paul.

"Hi, I need to ask you something important, do you have a minute?" he asked like he was talking to one of his office workers.

"I only have a minute, what do you want?" I asked, bracing myself for the hurt and pain I knew was coming.

"Hmm, I've never told anyone you left me except Betsy, and now my mother died yesterday…Please go with me to the funeral. That's all I'm asking. Stand beside me in that beautiful long black coat I bought you and wear the wine colored dress by the same designer. Bring that long silk slip I bought you from Tokyo. You'll look so beautiful and I'll be so proud. Please do this last thing for me and for my mother. She loved you so much. Please!" he begged.

"Yes, I'll go. When and where's the funeral?" I asked. I loved his mother also and it was the least I could do.

"It's at the little church in Egg Harbor. Her ashes will be scattered at her beach house later that day. People will be coming to the house to eat after the scattering. It'll be tomorrow," he said sounding like he was arranging a meeting.

"Tomorrow!" I shouted.

"You'll need to drive to Raleigh and catch a plane to Philly and a limo will bring you to the beach house. I've arranged everything. I'll bring up your dress and coat. You left a whole closet full of clothes."

"You were mighty sure I'd come," I said, wishing I'd said no. He was still telling me which slip to wear.

"Hoped, Meredith. I hoped you would come. You also left your things in the deposit box at the bank. I've gotten them out and will give them to you tomorrow," he said with a sigh.

"This is a round trip ticket right?" I asked.

"Yes, it's round trip. You'll be home before the weekend," he said, sounding like he knew Eric's routine, which creeped me out. It was only eight o'clock so I had time to pack, go to Lena's, and go with her to visit old Mr. Kincaid, then head out to Raleigh.

§

The nursing home visit didn't turn out as expected. He took one look at me and said evilly, "Well Rebecca, it's about time you got your ass home to take care of me. Now I can move out of this hell hole."

When I told him I wasn't Rebecca, but Meredith Winstead Smith-Hein, he started hollering. "Who are you? Who was your mother?"

I told him who my mother was and who my grandmother was since I didn't think he would remember my mother.

"I loved your grandmother. I didn't mean to hurt her. I told her I'd marry her, but she didn't want anything to do with me. Nothing I could do or say would make her love me. She told me if I didn't stop coming over she was going to call the sheriff on me."

Lena tried to hush him up while she hit the call bell to alert the nurses.

"I stopped bothering her like she wanted and married Virginia and eventually had three children by her, but I always loved your grandmother," he said, trying to get out of his chair.

"You're getting too upset. We'll talk about this another time," I said, trying to calm him.

"You know, I didn't plan to go that night. I hadn't bothered her for two whole years, but I started drinking and just decided I wanted her and I meant to have her. She didn't fight hard," he cried. "Afterward, I couldn't make her stop crying so I just left."

Lena and I just stood there. He was sobbing and cursing, and the nurses were trying to calm him down. Finally, we could shake off the shock of what we had heard and left.

"I told you he wasn't a nice man. I'm sorry you had to hear all that. I didn't know about it and if my mother did, she never said a word," Lena said. She looked as upset as I was.

"How old was my grandmother?" I asked.

"I bet she was forty-five at least. She had been a widow for more than ten years. Your mother had graduated from college and moved to Alexandria by then. She may have been married already. She got married soon after she moved," Lena said, looking at me then back to the road.

"Damn, poor lady. It sounded like he raped her," I said with disbelief.

"I've had to fight him off more than once myself. He was too old to do anything, but it still upset me. My girls are never around him. Bob would kill him if he touched the girls."

"Lena, I have to go to Cape May for my mother-in-laws funeral. I'm going to Raleigh this afternoon and flying to Philly. The funeral is tomorrow. Do you think Bob could stop by and feed the animals and milk the nanny? I'll be home Thursday so tomorrow is the only problem. I'll keep trying to contact Eric, and he may come home and take care of things."

"It's no problem. I'll do it. I've milked many a goat in my days. What do you do with the milk?" Lena asked, making the turn for her road. I could tell that our visit with Mr. Kincaid had really upset her. She drove a little wildly and sighed the whole way home.

We talked about using goat's milk and how she would teach me to make cheeses when I got home. We didn't talk about what had just happened with old Mr. Kincaid. It was just too horrible to wrap our minds around. I could tell Lena was as upset as I was.

"I got you covered. Have a safe trip," she said, parking her car in the yard next to mine. "Are you okay?" she asked, giving me a questioning look. "Do you want to come inside? I'll make some coffee."

"No. I have to get to Raleigh. I'm cutting it close as it is," I said, giving her a big hug.

Driving home, I realized I'd never had a close friend since high school. I hoped Lena and I would be good friends.

⤞⤝

I called Eric every hour, but his phone went to voice mail each time. I couldn't remember who he was working for this time, so I flew to Philly without contacting him. I tried one more time in the limo, but no luck. It was strange.

I went straight to the beach house. Paul met me at the door with some of his cousins and their spouses who obviously had been drowning their sorrow for awhile. I hugged them and said how sad it was, being here without Paul's mother.

"Thank you for coming. I know you were busy right now and this means a delay for the new museum opening," he lied, turning to make sure his cousins heard him. "I'll show you to your our room."

"There is no our room, Paul, and I mean it. I'll leave!" I said out of earshot of his cousins.

"Okay, you can sleep in my mother's room. Just wait until everyone is gone, please."

"Okay!"

"She left you her pearls. The good ones with the diamond bow clasp. Could you wear them tomorrow?" he said, moving on quickly.

"Sure. Now just leave me alone for a while. Just seeing you again has upset me."

⤞⤝

The funeral went well. The Episcopal music was soulful. You expected any minute for the roof of the chapel to open and heaven to send an angel to guide Paul's mother home. The scattering was at sunset on the beach in front of her home. It was chilly but beautiful. Birds sat offshore, bobbing in the water, watching as if they understood the short service and were taking part. Friends and family returned to the house for a late supper and more drinking. Around twelve, Paul and I were the only ones left at the house. The caterers had finished cleaning and

27

had left.

"Well Meredith, have you given any thought to coming home with me? I know you were hurt, but common sense should have kicked in by now."

"Actually I feel stronger every day. I am happy in the country," I said.

"Do you want to live your life in that rickety old house with an electrician for a husband? Is this the life you planned? I can't see you milking goats and feeding chickens with your beautiful hands. What about your career? How many museums do they have in that part of North Carolina?"

"Paul, the house is paid for. I just need taxes, utilities, and food. I'm planting a garden so food will be less and less every year. The museums can call me if they want me. Eric really makes enough for both of us. Thank you! How do you know what my hands are doing anyway?"

"I have my ways of knowing things," he said with his slimy grin.

"Well, then I guess you know I've never been happier," I said as I stomped into his mother's room. Thankfully he didn't try to sleep with me. I laid awake half the night worrying about what I would do if he tried. Hitting him over the head with my bedside lamp was the best I could come up with. I knew him, and he was holding back for some reason. Maybe it was Betsy or maybe he thought he would win in the end, and I'd come running back to him. In the morning, I felt like I only slept a few minutes instead of for the hours that had passed.

I'd been calling Eric over and over. I called Lena and asked if something had happened to him. She said she hadn't talked to him, but that my animals were fine. I told her I was leaving that morning. I planned to tell Paul I had to get back to my animals. I called the same limo that brought me. He said he would be there in an hour. I grabbed some coffee and found Paul sitting on the porch looking at the ocean.

"Paul I'm leaving soon. That was our deal," I said, looking at the ocean as Margie, Paul's mother must have done from this porch for years. The seagulls were diving here and there for breakfast. Margie inherited the house from her family. I knew Paul would sell it. He's never liked the mess sand makes. Hopefully someone will love it as much as Margie and her family did.

"Did you see the stuff from your safety deposit box?" he asked, looking up at me from his coffee cup. He was wearing shorts and a white t-shirt. He looked like he had gained some weight.

"I just packed it. I'll go through it at home. Thanks for remembering it and getting it out for me," I said, wondering what he was up to. I knew the letter from my grandmother was in there, or at least I did at the time I got it out of her safety deposit box. I was feeling guilty I hadn't made sure my grandmother was cared for after my mother died. I called twice a week, but that was all. I never came down to see if she was really okay. I'd felt bad and couldn't handle a note from the dead at the time.

"You're welcome. There was a note from your grandmother that you need to read before you go back to your life in Henderson. Pull it out and read it now," he all but ordered me.

"No! Good-bye, Paul, I'm so sorry about your mother. She was a good woman," I said, praying for the limo to get there.

"Well, I'll tell you what's in the letter," he said, following me into the kitchen. "Your mother never could have children. Your grandmother was raped and made pregnant by Robert Kincaid, Eric's dad, and your mother raised you as hers."

"What?"

"You've been shacking up with your half-brother. What a damn hoot that is. I've laughed and laughed," he said, doubling over with mirth. "You can come back if you want to, but the offer won't last long. Betsy is getting rather needy since you left. She's pregnant and I may have to marry her," he said. "Her father can make waves at my job and is insisting she get married before the baby is born. But I'd rather keep you."

❧❧

The limo took me to the airport in Philly. I was in a daze going through security, boarding and landing at RDU. I got my car and started home for Henderson. It took less than two hours. Eric's truck was in the yard and lights were on in the house when I drove up.

"Nice pearls," Eric said as I walked in the door. He was standing in the arch going to the living room. He could barely look at me.

"Thanks. Paul's mother left them to me. That was nice of her," I said, trying to get the courage I'd needed to talk to him about my grandmother's note. He looked so good in old but clean jeans, a white t-shirt with a much-washed flannel shirt worn as a jacket. His reddish brown hair was wavy and needed a trim. He was a couple of years younger than me and you could see it in his stance.

"I took care of the animals for you today. I wasn't sure you'd come back," he said, looking everywhere but at me. I lent my phone to my boss and he didn't get it back to me until today. One of his kids was sick.

"I saw where you and Lena had been calling over and over. I called you first and it went to voicemail. I called Lena and she said I needed to come home. You had some things to talk to me about. Are you going back to Paul?" he asked, looking at me for the first time.

"Oh, God no, I'll never go back to him," I said barely able to hold back my sobs.

"That's good, Meredith. So what can be so bad?" he asked.

"Eric, I've been thinking the whole way home. How I could possibly tell you what I've just learned? Your father raped my grandmother and got her pregnant with me. I'm really your half-sister."

"You're kidding. You're my sister? I've been having sex with my sister. This is so sick. I'm sorry, but I need to get out of here for a while. I'll be back, I promise. We'll sit down and talk this out, but right now I need space," He gave me a hug. A brotherly hug. Then he went out the front door. I could hear his old truck going down the road.

In an hour, he came back. "I'm ready to talk if you are," he said.

"I can't believe my mother didn't tell me. My grandmother left me a deathbed note, but she should have told me to my face. I didn't read the note. It was in my safety deposit box and Paul read it. He really enjoyed telling me what was in it, the buzzard. I still love you and not with a sisterly love. How do you feel? What do you want us to do?" I asked, sinking down on the couch. I was too weak to stand anymore. I could almost read his face and it was not what I wanted to read.

"Well, I was sick at first. I mean throw up sick. I felt I should have known somehow. I mean you look just like our grandmother's picture. Truthfully I don't remember her, and I never saw that picture. I did think you looked a lot like one of the twins and my sister Rebecca, a little."

"I had a nagging suspicion, especially after I saw Lena's daughter and the picture of the grandmother. I thought maybe we were cousins, but never did I think you were my brother," I said trying not to burst out in tears.

"I wanted to be here for you, but I'm not sure what I can do," he said, looking like his dog just got run over twice.

"I never had a brother or a sister so I don't know exactly how you feel, but it must be a strange feeling."

"I would never, and I mean never, make love to Rebecca. She looks so much like you. How could I not have had a hunch or a feeling? Meredith, I'm not sure I can ever make love to you again."

"I know. I can see it in your face. Let's go to bed and think about this in the morning. I can't make any plans right now. Can you hold your old sister one last night?"

"Sure, I'll hold you good and tight. I love you," he said quietly and I believed him. We slept in our clothes.

I woke up as Eric was zipping up his duffel bag. He was leaving. Tears pooled in my eyes as I pretended to be asleep. Maybe he would leave without saying anything. That was about all I could handle.

"I know you're awake. I see the tears," he said, sniffing as he sat on the side of the bed. "I'm so sorry, but this is too much for me to handle. I still love you and thought we would work out somehow, but I can't be loving on my own sister. I've got to go. Keep Tom for a while. I'll be back to get him once I can stand to look at you without wanting to take you to bed. I plan to be a good brother to you when I can. Take care. If you need anything, call Bob and Lena. They're family now."

He was gone, just like that. No kiss, no hug goodbye, not even a pat on the head. I heard his old truck start and speed down the road.

I just buried my head into my pillow and cried loud and hard. I lost my beautiful house in Alexandria, money, and a husband that came home every night. Maybe if I had pretended not to read those texts and emails, I'd be better off now. Betsy had Paul and all I had were two goats, three cats, a bunch of mice, and this old house. I was the good one. I didn't cheat. My will of steel wasn't doing me much good. I missed Eric horribly already.

My cell phone beeped. "Don't forget to feed the animals today." It was from Eric. No "I love you" or any sentiment at all. It was over.

When I went out that afternoon to feed the animals, I found that barn cat had delivered five kittens. Each one looked like it had a different dad. I watched her clean them and try to nurse them for hours. Sometimes I watched with wonderment and joy and other times tears of despair fell. Walking back to the house, I felt like someone had their arm around me and heard a quiet voice say, "Like you told Lena, he was what you needed at the time. You'll be okay."

Then, I felt the tiniest flutter in my belly.

About The Author

Sarah Sugg writes short stories, cozy mysteries, and novels. Steel Will is one of the short stories from The Mended Gown, which includes eight short stories with a much mended white antique gown wandering in and out of the stories. She has written four cozy mysteries featuring Daphne and Olive. They are two ladies in their sixties who enjoy gambling junkets in faraway cities, and often find themselves in the middle of murder mysteries. She has also written a mystery, Medals, about a box of religious medals that was purchased in an auction for five dollars. Death and mayhem followed. Her short stories have been published in blogs and anthologies.

Sarah lives in Raleigh, North Carolina and when she isn't writing, enjoys gardening and caring for her six grandchildren.

La Guaria Morada

Elizabeth Carroll

L iz Riley watched as the taxi driver pulled away. The warm Costa Rican sun beat down on her, and she shielded her eyes against its glare. She should have brought her sunglasses, but she'd been distracted this morning and left them sitting on the hotel bureau.

Turning away from the receding taxi, she fixed her eyes on the open space of land in front of her. The property was eighty-seven acres large, green and fertile, and unfortunately all hers. It was so quiet here, but then it had always been. Birds and breeze seemed to respect the sanctity of the place, for neither stirred. Only trails of butterfly vines creeping up the trellises marked the passage of time.

She wondered now if she should go back to the hotel and get her sunglasses. After all, she could always come back later, tomorrow, or even the next day. There was no need to hurry. There had never been a need to hurry.

Glancing over her shoulder, she saw that the cab had disappeared. She could call another one, should call another one, because coming here had been a mistake. Her hand went inside her tote to feel around for the phone, but her fingers brushed against the cold metal of the urn instead. She withdrew her hand and clutched the straps of the bag on her shoulder, her eyes staring straight ahead.

It wasn't supposed to be like this.

Renn was supposed to be here. This was to be their home. In fact, they had started the garden in which she now stood shortly after his marriage proposal. They had been so full of dreams and plans, and she was certain she had smiled a lot because seven years ago the world had seemed conquerable.

This land had been his pride and joy. She remembered how happy he'd been when the deed was signed, how enthusiastically he had worked in the garden. He never minded the sun that always kissed his skin or the dirt that got under his fingernails.

He should be here in the flesh, but he wasn't. He'd been dead for two long years, and there were still times when she had to remind herself of it. He'd only been twenty-eight at the time, and that was too young to die. She should know; she had just observed her own twenty-eighth birthday last month, and there was a lot of life still in front of her. He should be here to live it with her.

But no, he'd died of a headache. The medical professionals preferred the term "aneurism," but it was all the same to Liz. He'd assured her he would be all right, insisted that she go tend to her errands. He'd insisted; otherwise, she never would have left him alone.

Liz exhaled and shook her head. In front of her lay the garden she and Renn had planted together. In a world of fairness, the garden would have withered and died when Renn had, but no. It thrived, full of color, full of life. It felt as though God was poking fun at her. It made her angry.

To her right sat a run-down structure that had once stood as the workman's house. It wasn't quite as massive as a house; rather, it was like an over-sized shed with a door framed by two windows. In some ways, the building reminded her of a child's drawing, so square and simple was its design. The sight of it only stoked her fury. It had been a blemish on the landscape seven years ago, but Renn had only smiled and promised to tear it down. They could use the materials to start their own dream house, he'd reasoned. He'd believed whole-heartedly in recycling and taking care of the environment. Of course, he'd never gotten around to fulfilling that promise to her. There were a lot of things he'd never gotten around to.

Picking up a rock, Liz flung it at one of the windows. The pane of glass shattered, but she felt not the slightest bit of satisfaction. Maybe if she had a bulldozer and could flatten it to the ground…An eyesore seven years ago, the structure had now almost fallen in on itself. Butterfly vines had crept up and over the rotted wood, which only made her hate it all the more. It didn't belong here, it had never belonged here. What a cruel jab that it should still exist while Renn was no more.

Nothing about any of this was fair, including why she was here.

Turning her back on the building, she entered the gardens

through the overgrown trellis and walked down the little cobblestone path. A pair of stone benches sat in the center beside a dry, three-tiered fountain. Liz settled on one of the benches and sighed. It wasn't supposed to be like this. Renn was supposed to be here with her, on the bench, helping her plan their lives. Instead, God had taken him, just like He'd taken her parents, and she didn't know why. Maybe there was a lesson she was supposed to learn. Maybe she had been too selfish with her life.

Maybe that was it. She had become terribly comfortable in her life. She had no wants and no needs—other than Renn. She had made peace with her parents' death; after all, that had been thirteen years ago, but her husband? If only God would tell her what she was supposed to do, she would do it. She would do anything, give up anything, become anything if it would bring Renn back to her.

The brightness of the sunlight in the garden made her eyes water. She never went out without her sunglasses. Why on this day then had she left them behind? It was a beautiful day, the kind of day Renn would have liked – balmy and cloudless with a brilliant sun the likes of which could only be found in Costa Rica.

Tears slid out of her eyes, and she reached for the tissue in her bag. Her hand brushed against the urn again, but this time she did not pull away. The sunlight glinted off the metal as she removed it from her tote, and more tears fell as she cradled it against her. So light, so very, very light—it weighed less than twelve pounds altogether, and that was the cruelest cut of all. The essence that made up Renn Elmsby had been so much more than twelve measly pounds.

Liz cried on the bench in the garden. Renn had proposed to her in this very spot seven years ago. He had been sitting right beside her on the ground, and they had been talking about this and that and whatever when he had suddenly taken her hand in his and asked her. She remembered how serious his eyes had been, how frightened he must have been to think she'd say no.

She had never been able to say no to Renn—not that day, not any day.

Life with Renn had not been easy, and maybe she was partly to blame for that. She had tried to walk away when his addiction to painkillers had gotten too hard for both of them, but she hadn't been able to stay away. He was a part of her. They should have had longer. They had fought the demon between them and won. Renn had cleaned up his act, and they had started to move forward into a future that was not to be.

Gradually, the tears she didn't know she still had in her began to dry. Her face was now a wet mess, but she made no move to clean it. Instead, she settled the urn on the bench beside her, her fingers lingering over the knob on the lid. She should have brought him home a long time ago.

"Hey, you," she said softly. "We finally made it back, didn't we?" Once upon a time, they had dreamed of building a house right up the hill from where she now sat. She had even envisioned a jicaro tree in the front yard, a tire swing hanging from one of its branches for their children to play on. None of that had happened, of course, and the regret swelled inside her chest and threatened to suffocate her.

"I'm sorry it took me so long to get you here," she said. Her voice shook with emotion, so she stopped and took a deep breath instead. She dug the toe of her shoe into the ground until she felt stronger.

"I was afraid to come back. It's hard to be here without you. It's hard everywhere, but especially here." She exhaled. "I guess I didn't want Costa Rica to become a place of grief, you know? I have enough places like that back home in the States."

She paused and glanced around. "I closed up the house in LA for a while. I'm going to be living in Vermont now. It's nice there and quiet and pretty. You'd like it. Everything is so lush and fertile. I built a house, but don't worry—it's environmentally friendly and energy efficient."

Renn would have liked that. The thought made her smile, and for a long while she said little else. What was there to say, really? Renn was gone, and for whatever reason Liz had not been allowed to go with him. She didn't know how to feel about that. The last two years had felt like an eternity, yet she truly believed she was starting to rise out of the ashes her life had become after his death. Was it a good thing that she should be getting on with her life? She didn't know.

Maybe Renn would. He had come to her once before. Nearly a year ago, she had awakened in the middle of the night to find a storm raging outside. Her bedroom, in contrast, had been warm and full of light, and in the middle of that light had been her Renn. He had spoken to her, told her that he loved her, that he would always love her, and that he wanted her to be happy. He had told her he would wait for her.

She'd never told a soul about that. She didn't want people speculating as to whether it had been a dream or a vision or a grief-induced hallucination. She knew he had been there, knew it with every fiber of her being. He was watching out for her, and that thought had buoyed her spirits enough to get her back down to Costa Rica.

Maybe he was watching her now.

"I'm trying," she said after a long silence, "to do what you told me. I'm trying to be happy. I started the organization we talked about, and I named it after you. The Renn Elmsby Homes for the Homeless Project." She could almost see him grimace, and she shrugged apologetically. "I know. You're probably thinking it's presumptuous, and maybe it is, but I don't want them forgetting you, forgetting what you stood for. You were so much more than…than this." Her fingers closed around the top of the urn, and her eyes dampened a second time. "Truthfully? I really don't know how to do this without you."

She looked away. For a moment, the gardens were a blur of yellow, white, pink, and purple. Blinking back the tears, Liz saw that the splotches of color were actually flowers growing as freely as you please. She hadn't noticed them before, but now they drew her attention, especially the purple ones.

La guaria morada.

Liz stood from her bench, a sense of awe taking the place of loss. The orchids, Costa Rica's national flower, seemed to have chosen their own bed at the base of a cluster of trees. Here they made a sea of lilac, plum, and violet. Renn had always insisted on giving her a single bloom nestled in a bunch of tulips, her favorite flower. She had almost forgotten about that. It felt as though she had found a long lost friend.

Crossing the greenery, the urn cradled against her, she found a bare spot beneath a tree covered with flowers and sat. The silver urn looked oddly pretty nestled in the flowers where she placed it. Careful not to flatten any of the orchids, she lay back on the ground and closed her eyes. The sun was warm on her face. She took a deep breath, but there was no fragrance on the air.

"You can't smell it, Angel."

Renn's voice, pulled from the recesses of her mind, sounded as real and close as if he was lying right beside her. Her heart leaped, but she kept her eyes closed so as not to break the spell.

"Its scent is full of dreams that have yet to be fulfilled," Renn told her from long ago. A tear slid out of the corner of her eye as she remembered, and she pushed her own dreams out so that the petals of the orchids could catch them and hold them and maybe one day make them come true.

"They say it also brings luck and good fortune." His voice dropped to a whisper near her ear, and for a moment, Liz thought she felt his breath against her skin. "It evokes peace and love and hope for the future. Your future, Angelita. Seas feliz."

Something brushed against her cheek like a kiss, and a chill ran down her spine. She opened her eyes and sat up suddenly. "Renn?"

Out in the garden, heads of pink, yellow, and white swayed serenely, and overhead leaves rustled with their own music. A gentle breeze stirred la guaria morada so that each flower brushed against her skin. It felt like kisses. Renn's kisses.

Yes, he had been here. She felt it, just as she had that night a year ago when he had come to her and told her the same thing—Seas feliz, Angelita. Be happy, Little Angel—his nickname for her.

She heard the whispers now in the sway of flowers in the garden they had planted together, in la guaria morada so full of unfulfilled dreams. He was here. He wanted to be here. And he wanted happiness for her.

Getting to her feet, Liz picked up the urn and made her way back to the stone bench. The time had come. Renn was going home.

She stood on the bench and removed the top of the urn. As if on cue, the wind picked up slightly and carried the ashes she shook free across the land that she and Renn had once dreamed of calling home.

"Te amo, Renn," she called out as the urn emptied. She would miss him always, but he would never be far from her. She knew that now.

When the last of the ash had blown away from her, Liz climbed down and set the urn beneath the bench. A feeling akin to relief filled her. She was going to be okay. Renn had given that to her, and she hoped she had given it right back.

With a smile more genuine than any she'd had in a long while, Liz Riley turned and headed out of the garden. Costa Rica belonged to Renn. Her life waited for her back in the States.

Seas feliz, Angelita.

She thought now she just might have a chance.

About The Author

As a girl who always had her head in the clouds, Elizabeth Carroll knew she was destined to become a writer. She also knew she would most likely develop an addiction to sweet tea, that she would enjoy all kinds of music, and that her hobbies would include putting puzzles together, reading, baking, and spending time with her family. What she didn't know was that she would become wife to Charlie and mommy to Wesley, the two greatest fellas in the world. She also was surprised to learn that she actually likes yoga and exercise, that she would find a career in teaching, and that Teenage Mutant Ninja Turtles would become her go-to cartoon of choice.

In between all the knowing-and-discovering that goes on in her life, she managed to graduate from UNC-Wilmington with a Master's degree in creative writing. She then began a career teaching and writing. Her first two novels, The Secret Keeper and The Convergence, are part of a young adult fantasy fiction series and were self-published with Wheatmark, Inc. The third book, The Gateway, will be available this summer.

Allagash

Elizabeth Hein

August 1985
Northern Maine Wilderness

It was supposed to be their last great adventure before starting college in the fall. A backwoods canoe trip down the Allagash River sounded like fun. When Greg and Snig asked Midge to come with them, she imagined ten days of singing around the campfire with her best friend, leisurely paddling along the river while watching moose and eagles, and reveling in nature's majesty. She didn't anticipate Snig ditching her to spend time with her boyfriend or their guide forcing the stronger paddlers to take turns pulling her down the river.

By the sixth day of hard paddling through ceaseless rain, Midge vowed to never get in a canoe or go camping again. Whenever she flexed her fingers, the blisters on her palms reopened. Her sleeping bag was waterlogged, her clothes were soggy, and she had mosquito bites on top of her mosquito bites. Nature be damned. She wanted to go home, take a warm bath, and then sleep for a week.

The first five men assigned to accompany her ignored her except to bark at her to paddle harder. Eustace was different. While they worked their way down that morning's section of the river, they chatted about her concerns about starting college in the fall and his fears about finishing his Ph.D. and becoming a microbiology professor. He was nervous about standing at the front of the lecture hall, rather than sitting in one of the desks. Midge assured him he would make a great professor.

The rain finally stopped the late morning of the sixth day. Their river guide sent a message back along the line of canoes that they would be pulling out at the portage near the collapsed bridge. Originally, they planned to carry the canoes around the dangerous rapids and camp further downriver; however, the group needed a sunny afternoon to rest and dry out their things.

By the time the message got to Midge and Eustace at the back of the line, the sun was casting long shadows across the river and Midge had a crush on Eustace. He was ideal -- a golden mane of hair contained in a low ponytail, chiseled features, dreamy blue eyes, and completely unavailable. Their river guide, on the other hand, loathed him. When he realized the gorgeous Eustace and dumpy Bradley were more than just friends, he stopped talking to them and turned his nose up whenever they offered to help with anything. When Midge overheard the guide mutter something about the two of them spreading AIDS around the campsite, she bit her tongue, resisted the urge to hit the guide over the head with her shovel, and stalked off to dig a latrine. She was trying to control what her mother called her "angry spells" and failing. Days of aching shoulders, no sleep, and wet clothes had pushed Midge to her breaking point.

When Midge and Eustace finally reached the campsite, she was disappointed their day together was over. She expected him to dump her as soon as they lifted the canoe out of the water. Instead, Eustace carried Midge's gear up to the clearing where the group would set up for the communal meal and asked, "Where are you going to pitch your tent for the night?"

"I don't know. Over there, I guess." She blushed and pointed vaguely to the woods. "My tent leaks wicked bad. Last night, I didn't even bother setting it up. I just put a tarp down and slept under my canoe."

"Wait here for a sec," he said. "I'll go put my stuff down then help you find a place to dry your stuff out."

"Thanks," Midge said. She looked around to see if anyone had seen this gorgeous specimen of male kindness paying attention to her. She watched Eustace walk a few yards beyond the clearing to a yellow dome-shaped tent that had obviously been constructed by someone who had been camping more than once before. He exchanged a few words with his boyfriend, Bradley, before ducking into the tent and re-emerging with a bundle in his hand. They both walked back to Midge.

"I hear all your stuff got wet," Bradley said. He handed Midge a rolled-up sleeping bag and a baggie filled with half a roll of dry toilet paper. Midge resisted the urge to hug him. Her toilet paper had disintegrated into a pile of mush after the first day of rain. She had been using leaves ever since and praying that she didn't wind up with poison ivy on her backside.

"We can't have you being a damsel in distress. Come on," Eustace said with a grin. He pointed to an enormous pine tree two hundred yards from the clearing. "Let's set up your tent under that big tree. If the rain holds off, maybe it will dry out overnight." Eustace ducked under the veil of green and stood up near the pale trunk. A thick bed of dry needles covered the ground under the wide branches. "Oh yeah, there is plenty of room under here for one girl. Or, are you bunking with your friend?"

"I'm supposed to be sharing with Snig, but once it started raining and we realized the tent leaks, she's been sharing with her boyfriend."

Bradley smirked and raised an eyebrow behind his horn-rimmed glasses.

"I'm trying not to judge. Greg's not that bad of a guy, really." She stopped trying to defend Greg and Snig's behavior. She didn't approve of their relationship. Midge was shocked when she came back from her summer job as a camp counselor to find out Snig and Greg were having sex. She thought Snig was smarter than that.

Bradley and Midge pushed through the branches and joined Eustace. Together, the three of them unrolled her sodden tent and shook it out. The two men ended up attaching the roof line of the tent to a low branch with a few bungee cords so it didn't sag under its own weight. "I think they're planning to make a big stew later. Make sure you get some before it's all gone. You need to stay warm." She thanked them with a lump in her throat. Their little kindnesses had gone a long way to making her feel less alone in the woods. Bradley had given her a sympathetic pat on the shoulder before they left her to unpack the rest of her things.

She took a few minutes to hang her wet clothes over the low branches, looped her dripping sleeping bag over her shoulders, and climbed the tree. Ten feet off the ground, there was a slight breeze. She hung the sleeping bag over a bare branch. With any luck, she would sleep inside her sleeping bag that night instead of wrapped in her emergency blanket like a giant burrito. Midge straddled a sturdy branch and leaned back against the tree. It was quite comfortable. She wondered if she could sleep up there if it started to rain again.

The late afternoon sun penetrated the branches of the pine tree. She closed her eyes and enjoyed the warmth on her legs and feet. After days of rain and endless paddling, it was nice to simply relax. Her aching limbs felt heavy. She braced herself more securely with an arm slung over one branch and a foot wedged between two others. She would feel stupid if she fell asleep and tumbled out of the tree. She nodded off to the wind in the trees and the group's voices in the distance until one distinct voice woke her. Snig was somewhere close by and angry.

She peered through the branches. It was still bright out. However, a rosy glow was growing behind the pines along the opposite river bank. She stood up and hopped from one branch to another around the strong trunk. Whenever she climbed a pine tree, which was infrequently, she marveled at how like a spiral staircase the radiating branches were. She and Snig had once hidden in the big tree at the corner of their yard for hours during a block-wide game of hide and seek. To keep Midge from fidgeting, Snig had explained how conifers grew in a spiral configuration. Midge had wanted to call ollie-ollie-in-come-free when it got dark. However, Snig had refused to surrender after hiding for so long. She did climb down and return with a big flashlight to guide Midge down after they'd won the game. Now Midge was glad they'd had that experience together. She felt totally comfortable standing on a branch twenty feet off the ground.

On the other side of the tree, she saw Snig storming toward the campsite with Greg in hot pursuit. He grabbed her by the arm and spun her around. His face was flushed and his chest was heaving from the run. "Get rid of it," he yelled.

Midge couldn't see Snig's face through the branches. She moved down a branch to get a better view and saw Snig's long black braid quivering on the back of her t-shirt. Her shoulders were shaking

"Oh Christ," Midge whispered. "What did that loser do to make her cry?"

Midge and Snig had been best friends since the first day of kindergarten. Midge could only remember Snig crying three times -- when she fell roller skating and broke her wrist when she came in second in the Math Olympiad, and when her grandmother died. She usually hid her emotions behind the glossy wall of her intellect.

"I don't even know if there is an it to get rid of," Snig sobbed. "You asked me what was bothering me and, stupid me, I told you."

"You don't understand. I'm not like you. I don't have a rich daddy to take care of me." Greg let go of her arm and stepped back. "You can afford to make mistakes. I can't."

"This isn't about money. Or my dad. It's about you and me."

Midge considered pelting Greg with pinecones but didn't want to alert them to her being in the tree. She hated the way he taunted Snig about her family. He'd picked up on Snig's resentment toward her father for throwing money at her instead of spending time with her, and picked at it like a scab.

Greg turned toward the river and rubbed his forehead with the back of his hand. "How can I know if it's even mine?"

Snig lunged forward and pushed Greg. He didn't have time to put his arms out to break his fall. He flew face-first into the trunk of a small maple tree. He righted himself and wiped some blood from a scrape on his cheek. "What the hell? You could have hurt my hands. I'm going to be a surgeon."

"You're going to be a dead man if you don't take that back," Snig snarled. Midge was relieved to see she'd slipped back into a much more comfortable emotion -- rage.

He held his hands up and backed away another step. "Okay. I'm sorry. I didn't mean that. I'm just really freaking out right now."

"Like I'm not? I'm supposed to leave for MIT in two weeks."

"That's different." He dabbed at his face with the hem of his shirt and frowned at the blood that came off. "My dad says it's wrong for them to even take your father's money. You'll just get married anyway."

Snig's body vibrated with rage. "What is his problem? It's 1985, girls go to college now. We're not supposed to all be barefoot and pregnant anymore." Snig put her hand on her belly. "What are we going to do?"

"We aren't going to do anything. If you're such a smarty pants, you figure it out." Greg dabbed at his face again. "My dad said I should never have gone out with you. I'm going to be a doctor. I can't marry someone like you."

"Don't get ahead of yourself, buddy." Midge let out a quiet cheer as Snig shoved him again. He braced himself this time and still went flying. At six feet tall, Snig was stronger and faster than most of the young men she competed against in their fencing club. "I'm not asking you to marry me. I'm just telling you I missed my period. I'm probably just anemic from eating nothing but granola bars for the last few days." She turned to walk away, then stopped. She spun around again. "Wait a minute, what do you mean someone like me? What exactly don't you like about me?"

"Nothing, baby," he said reaching out for her. "You're awesome."

Snig backed away out of his reach. "No, really. What's wrong with me?" She bounced on her toes like a boxer. "Am I too tall? Too skinny? Too pretty?"

"It's nothing like that, Snig." Greg stepped forward, dangerously close to her clenched fists. "I don't know. I guess you're too much like me. That's why I like you so much. You'd make an awesome doctor."

"Huh?"

"You're just not the kind of girl that would be a good doctor's wife. Look at your parents. I can't spend my life with someone who's smarter than me, no matter how pretty she is."

Midge gasped and almost fell out of the tree. Greg had pierced the chinks in Snig's armor, her extraordinary intelligence and her parents. For most of her childhood, Snig had watched her parents maneuver their professional ambitions and family obligations like pieces around a chess board. She was their pawn and the game usually ended in a stalemate.

Midge scooted further out on her branch to better see her friend's face. Snig was just as liable to punch Greg at this moment as dissolve in tears. Snig wiped a tear from her cheek. "I understand. Forget I said anything. I'll take care of it."

"Come on, Snig. Don't be like that?"

"No, I understand. You know what you need. And, you're right. I am not it." Snig flipped her braid over her shoulder like a cape. "Go off to school. Study hard. Meet some sweet girl who will put you through medical school while teaching second grade."

Tears streamed down Midge's cheeks as she watched her best friend turn to walk away with her head held high. She could tell Snig was shattered. She had allowed Greg into her heart and now he was breaking it. Greg stood there and watched her walk away into the woods. When she was gone, he picked up a branch and pummeled the little maple tree until the branch broke into a thousand splinters.

Midge broke off a dead branch and threw it at Greg. It hit him on the shoulder. He spun around and yelled, "What the hell?"

She descended from her perch and pushed through the branches of the tree.

"Where did you come from?"

"I can't believe you." Midge kicked him in the shin. "You just threw away the best girlfriend you're ever going to have. I hope you find your perfect little doormat of a girl and she ends up stomping on your heart, you ass!"

She turned and ran after Snig. She was heading toward an old house in the distance. Half of the roof was missing and all the paint had flaked off the bare clapboards. Their river guide had said something about how there had once been a ranger station there until the bridge had washed away. Apparently the ranger station had been abandoned too. The two-story house was bigger than Midge thought a ranger station would be. She envisioned them as being tiny shacks in the woods where a lone man hoarded guns and hunched over his radio. This was a family's house with the remnants of a large kitchen garden to one side and an inviting front step. She wondered what happened to the ranger and his family after the station was abandoned. Were they swept away in the flood that took out the bridge or had they moved to the national park at Presque Isle? Midge imagined what it must have been like for the family that lived way out there in the Maine woods and how much they must have enjoyed the occasional beaver trapper that stopped in or the excitement they must have felt when a group of loggers would stop there before breaking down their log rafts to portage them around the rapids.

She lost sight of Snig. She was tempted to call out for her until she saw Bradley, Eustace, and a woman with a loose bun walking toward the house from the left. Midge didn't want to bring attention to Snig if she was crying somewhere nearby. She waited behind a tree for them to pass. If felt wrong that they were laughing together. The woman said, "We might be able to dig up some potatoes or a carrot. This soil is amazing."

"I wonder if they planted any raspberries or high bush blueberries," Eustace said. He sounded like a kid on a scavenger hunt rather than a microbiology professor. "They would self-propagate."

Bradley carried a short collapsible shovel in one hand. "I don't know. It doesn't look like anyone's lived here in a long time. Wouldn't the vegetables poop out after a few seasons?"

"It has been a long time," the woman replied. "They wouldn't have been using the new strains of seed that produce tons of big fruits, but need fertilizer to keep going. I doubt we'll find any tomatoes, but we might find a few puny root vegetables." The woman pointed to a spot in the yard and Bradley started digging around. A few other people joined them and sifted the disturbed soil through their fingers for treasure. Eustace and another man walked around the back of the house.

Suddenly, Midge heard a sharp cry. She couldn't tell where it had come from until Bradley dropped the shovel and ran toward the back of the house. The woman was at his heels and yelling for help.

Snig must have heard the yelling as well because by the time Midge had scrambled through the undergrowth, Snig was running toward her. When she saw Midge, she yelled, "Get some rope! As much as you can. And find the river guide."

Snig turned and ran back to the house. Midge paused only a second before turning toward the river. The clearing was only a few hundred feet away at this point. The river guide was standing in the shallows rinsing out equipment. The sound of the rushing water must have been too loud for him to have heard Snig yelling for help. Midge waved her arms as she ran. She was out of breath when she finally got his attention.

"There's been an accident!"

The guide peppered her with questions she couldn't answer.

"I don't know. All I know is they need rope. Lots of rope!"

The guide told one of the others to gather up anything that resembled a rope and help Midge carry it to the house. He grabbed a coil of nylon rope from the emergency kit in his canoe and took off running. He yelled names as he sped out of the clearing. Several people came crashing through the underbrush. "Who's hurt?" they demanded. "Is it Renee?"

"I don't think so," Midge gasped. She felt lightheaded from running. "I think it was Eustace or Bradley. I couldn't see." She looked around and grabbed the towline from the front of one of the canoes. "Come on, help me untie these lines. They might be useful."

By the time they got the lines untied and ran into the woods, the yelling had stopped. The guide, Snig, and several others were standing in a circle behind the house. Bradley lay on the ground with half his body in a hole. He called Eustace's name over and over. Greg was holding his feet so he didn't slide in.

Midge stood on her tiptoes and peered into the hole. It was no more than three feet across. Below a foot or so of dirt, she could see the stone and mortar walls of an old well. Jagged pieces of sod and wood hung over the edges. Midge's stomach flipped when she saw the two places that Eustace had grabbed at the grass as he'd fallen.

The man beside her dropped the pile of rope he had in his arms. "What happened?"

The woman with the bun lifted her face. Her expression was blank. "We were looking for vegetables and he saw some blueberries ... and then he was gone."

"Eustace!" Bradley screamed again.

Someone turned to the guide. "What do we do now? What can we do?"

He seemed to shake off his initial shock. "Umm, first we need to contact the closest ranger and get medical help."

"You said this used to be the ranger station," Greg said from where he held on to Bradley's ankles. "Where is it now?"

The guide turned around and pointed into the woods. "Five or six miles that way." He had lost his swagger and looked more like the young kid that he was.

"I'll go," a girl who looked like she was around sixteen said. "We run that far all the time in cross country practice."

The guide's shoulders relaxed. "That would be great." He unhooked a compass from his belt loop. "Head due east for about a mile until you hit the logging road. Take that south until you get to the ranger station or see a truck. Have them call the ambulance in Presque Isle."

The girl took the compass and ran into the woods. No one said anything, but Midge could see from their faces that they were all thinking the same thing. It was stupid to send a young girl running into the woods at dusk alone.

Greg pulled Bradley back from the edge of the hole by his feet. He crawled forward on his belly as if Eustace had fallen through a hole in ice rather than into a hole in the ground. He hung his head over the hole.

"How deep is this well?"

"It's not a well for water. It's a dry well," Snig said from a few feet back. She walked around the hole and kneeled near the edge. Midge held her breath. She was worried the ground would give out under her friend. "Do any of you macho men have a little flashlight on that utility thingy hanging from your belts?"

One of the guys eased up beside her and handed her his pen light. Clods of dirt fell into the hole. The crowd gasped in unison as he jumped back. Midge stepped forward and grabbed the back of her shirt. If Snig fell in, Midge was either going to stop her or go in with her.

Snig put her hand up and shushed them. "Did anyone hear a splash?" She looked up. "Did anyone hear a splash when he fell?"

The woman with a bun shook her head violently. "No...I don't know...all I heard was Eustace screaming."

Bradley raised his head from where he was laying on the ground. His eyes were crazed with grief. "I didn't hear any splash. I heard a thump." The woman with a bun went to him and put her arm around his shoulders.

Snig shone the light into the hole. Its beam quickly dissipated. "I can see something. Get me a rock."

One of the others ran over to where Bradley had been digging and returned with a rock the size of a baseball.

"Now everyone, shut up!" She dropped the rock into the hole. They instantly heard the rock hit something at the bottom. There was no splash.

"Good," Snig said with a wide smile. "Not deep at all."

"Deep enough!" A voice echoed from the hole. "Stop throwing rocks."

"Eustace!" Bradley scrambled over to the hole.

Greg grabbed the back of his shirt and pushed him flat on the ground to keep him from sliding in. "Careful, the ground might not be stable at the edge."

Snig shone the light around until the beam hit the tip of Eustace's upstretched hand. "Are you hurt?"

"Yes." He paused as if forming words was difficult. "I think my legs are broken." There was an edge of panic in Eustace's voice. "I can feel a lot of blood with my hand, but it doesn't hurt."

"We'll get you out," the guide yelled down.

"Quickly," Greg said. His cheeks were flushed. He looked more excited than upset. "He'll probably lose consciousness soon."

One of the men performed a complicated series of knots in the nylon rope to form two large loops at the end of the rope. He threw the looped end into the hole and shouted. "Put your arms through the loops."

"Shouldn't we wait for the ranger?" another voice asked. "He's hurt. We shouldn't move him."

"We can't leave him down there!" Bradley screamed. One of the others grabbed his arm as he lunged for the hole.

Greg backed away from the hole and motioned for the others to join him out of earshot of Bradley. With their heads together, he said, "We need to get him out of there. He can't feel his legs so his spine is probably already broken. We can't break it more." His eyes danced in the same way they did when they played chess. "We need to get him out of that hole before he goes into cardiac arrest or something. I can give him CPR once he's out if I have to."

They all nodded in agreement. "Okay, let's do this."

When they returned to the edge of the hole, the guide yelled down, "All set, down there?"

"I got the rope over my shoulders...feel like puking."

"Come on," Greg said. He grabbed the rope. "We need to do this. Now."

They all took a spot along the rope like in a game of tug-of-war. Bradley laid on the ground with his arms hanging in the hole. Snig and Greg were closest to the hole so they could grab Eustace as soon as he was in reach. The men pushed Midge and the woman with a bun to the side as they lined up behind Snig. They ran to the back of the group and picked up the last bit of rope.

"Okay, on three, pull. One...two...three!" They all started pulling.

"Oh, crap!" Eustace yelled.

"He's off the bottom. I can see his head and one hand," Bradley said. "Hang on, Eustace. We'll get you out."

They pulled again and took two steps back from the hole.

"How much further?" the guide asked.

"He's still at least six feet down there."

They took two more steps back. The rope bit into Midge's palms where she had wrapped it around her hands. Her back and shoulders trembled with the strain.

"Only a few more feet," Bradley called. "He's not hanging on to the rope anymore. I think he passed out,"

"Okay, we need to get him out of there. Now!" Greg shouted. "Big step. One, two, three!" They all took a big step back.

Suddenly, Midge was on her back and someone was on top of her. Bradley was screaming. Greg was screaming. Snig was screaming. Everyone was screaming. Midge freed herself from the person on top of her in time to see several of the men pulling Bradley's legs. Bradley was holding on to the snapped rope. The rest of the group ran to the side of the hole and pulled Bradley up, then hauled Eustace out of the hole. His body was limp. He wasn't moving.

Midge couldn't watch. She turned and saw Snig sitting on the ground with her feet splayed out in front of her. Her eyes were frozen wide and she was breathing heavily. The front of her shirt was covered with blood. The tips of two of her fingers lay in her lap. Snig held her right hand over the place where the fingers had been. Blood oozed through her fingers.

Midge felt like she was going to faint until her camp counselor training kicked in. She took a deep breath and crawled over to Snig.

"The rope broke," Snig said. Her voice sounded far away. Her eyes started rolling back in her head.

"Snig!" Midge slapped her cheek like she had seen people do in movies. "Stay with me here!" She pulled off her canvas belt and tied it around Snig's forearm as a tourniquet. She yelled over her shoulder for help. Only the woman with a bun came.

"Take off your shirt," Midge commanded. "Turn it inside out and wrap the fingers in it." The woman turned green. However, she did what she was told. In the meantime, Midge removed her own shirt and wrapped it around Snig's hand. "I'm sorry, this is gonna hurt wicked bad. I need to stop the bleeding."

"Bleeding. Stop the bleeding." Snig seemed to register what Midge was saying and nodded. Midge wrapped the shirt as tightly as she could and tied the sleeves together in a knot. Snig was crying by now. The initial shock of the injury was wearing off. When Midge was done, Snig looked over her shoulder at the group of men trying to revive Eustace.

"Is he dead?"

"I don't know. I'm taking care of you right now."

"The rope broke. I was trying to pull him up but then--" Snig's eyes widened. She looked away at the trees crowding around them. Midge yanked on the belt to tighten the makeshift tourniquet. Snig was still losing blood and she had no idea how long it would take the ranger to get there.

"Midge," Snig whispered. "The rope. It was cutting into our hands."

Midge held up her palms to show Snig the red lines where the rope had bit into her hands.

Snig's eyes were crazed as she looked across the yard at Greg's back. "He let go. Midge, it was hurting his precious hands."

Midge convinced one of the men to go back to the first aid kit and get her some ice packs to keep the severed pieces of Snig's fingers cold.

She wasn't sure if a doctor could reattach them. They always seemed to on television if they were kept on ice. While they waited for him to come back, Midge stood up and went over to where Greg and Bradley were bending over Eustace. They were pounding on his chest and doing mouth-to-mouth resuscitation. The others had retreated several yards away. It was hard to look at Eustace's broken body. That's all that was left of him now, a body. Midge bowed her head and said a prayer thanking God for letting her know Eustace for that one day and in hope that he would find peace in Heaven. She allowed grief to fill her heart for a few more minutes, then turned to attend to the task at hand. She returned to Snig and helped her move to the back steps of the abandoned house so she could lean against the railing. Snig smiled at Midge and wiggled her thumb and forefinger. "Should you loosen the belt. My other fingers are turning blue."

"The ranger should be here soon and then we can get you to a hospital."

Snig closed her eyes. Her lips were pale, but blood had stopped blooming through Midge's t-shirt.

When the other camper returned with the ice packs and a plastic bag, he brought Midge some gauze and a clean t-shirt. Midge blushed as she took it. She had been so intent on saving Snig's fingers that she'd forgotten she was wearing nothing but her bra. She pulled the t-shirt over her head. It was too tight, but it would do.

Now that the initial crisis had passed, tears welled up in Midge's eyes. The enormity of what had happened hit her. Eustace was dead and Snig was seriously injured. She knew the ranger was on his way but was he going to be able to do? Would he have already called an ambulance? Could an ambulance even get to them? What if that girl got lost and the ranger wasn't coming at all? Then what would they do? They couldn't take a body with them down the river. Would they split up and send someone else for help?

Snig nudged Midge's knee with her own. "Pisser of a day, huh?"

"Peachy."

"I saw you in the tree."

"Sorry." Midge nudged her back. "I'm really sorry about Greg."

"Duly noted." In those two words, Snig was saying - I know you weren't eavesdropping, I know you told me that Greg was lousy boyfriend material, and I know you're on my side.

"Okay then," Midge replied. "Prop your hand on my shoulder so it's above your heart."

They sat quietly while the other people slowly drifted back to their campsites. The sun was going down. There was only so long they could stand around and stare at a dead body. At one point, the aroma of fish roasting over a wood fire wafted over Midge. Life was going on near the river.

By the time the ranger and the runner crashed through the woods on an ATV, only Midge, Snig, Greg, Bradley, and the guide remained in the yard. The men had a quick conversation over Eustace's body. Bradley started wailing anew when the ranger went back to the ATV and returned with a body bag.

Only then did the ranger make his way over to Snig. "Hey, little lady. Did you hurt your hand?"

"I severed two digits if that's what you mean. The pieces are in that bag."

"Is there an ambulance on the way?" Midge asked. "She's lost a lot of blood."

Greg pushed Midge aside and grabbed Snig's injured hand. She flinched. "I can wrap the wound."

Midge shoved Greg out of the way. "Back off! This is your fault. You don't get to touch her."

The ranger inspected the tourniquet and Midge's handiwork. "Someone was a Girl Scout," he said dismissively.

"Step off, buddy," Midge retorted. "She could have bled to death for all these idiots cared." The river guide had the decency to look ashamed. "Did you call for an ambulance to come over from Quebec?"

"I've got the medevac guys on standby," the ranger replied. He sized up the clearing. "You think we need to get them in here?"

"I don't think so," Greg said from a safe distance behind the ranger. "I can bandage her up until the ambulance gets here."

"No," Snig said. Her eyelids were fluttering. Now that the ranger was there and help was definitely on its way, she was fading. Midge was worried that she was going into shock. "What good is having money if you can't spend it," Snig slurred. "Get on your CB and call my father. Tell him to send the helicopter to come get his little girl."

About The Author

Elizabeth Hein writes women's fiction with a bit of an edge. Her novels explore the role of friendship in the lives of adult women and themes of identity. Her novel, *How To Climb The Eiffel Tower*, examines the redemptive power of friendship in the face of cancer, where her first novel, *Overlook*, highlights the darker side of suburban life. Her third novel, *Escape Plan*, will be released in 2016. She is currently working on a novella and another novel. Elizabeth enjoys interacting with her readers, and can be found on Facebook, Twitter, Google+, and her blog.

Elizabeth Hein grew up in an extended family of storytellers. Her childhood was filled with excellent food and people loudly talking over each other. After earning a degree in psychology and philosophy, she and her husband embarked on the adventure of parenting their two beautiful daughters. Motherhood led Elizabeth to start a small business, home school one of her daughters for several years, and learn more about competitive swimming than she ever thought possible. She and her husband now live in North Carolina.

The Widow's Daughter

R Leanda

I was lonely.

At five in the morning, I left Baltimore wearing my funeral suit and carrying a small overnight bag. I thought that I would reconnect with my North Carolina relatives during our cousin's funeral, and stay at a nearby hotel for the night. In fact, I thought it possible that I would stay a couple of days, reminiscing with them about when we were children. Maybe they would even be interested in making the drive out to the country to see what was left of my parent's old place.

I found myself sweating in my dark suit, surrounded by strangers who were genuinely grieving for one of their own. I realized that I'd made a big, selfish mistake. The funeral wasn't supposed to be a family reunion. Apparently, my deceased cousin was a good guy and he had a nice, well-attended funeral.

I wondered if mine would be.

My two grown children didn't live close by, so I got a ten-minute call once every couple of weeks. The divorce happened three years earlier, and I didn't retain custody of our mutual friends. My closest friend was in an Alzheimer's home, and he walked in a large circle all day. Once in a while, I held his hand and walked with him. All the rest of my friends were business friends and my retirement had happened at the end of the previous year. They disappeared with the ice cream cake.

I was grieving for my own family and social connections, not my deceased cousin. Instead of joining the rest of the stranger-mourners for a late lunch, I decided to drive by myself out to my mother's farm, even though I knew the small farmhouse wasn't there anymore.

When I was little, I remember Raleigh being a long way away.

However, it took me less than an hour to get to the Methodist church where my parents, Charles and Ida Lee Smith, are buried.

After I had visited their graves, I decided to drive by the old farm, even though I knew our little house was long gone. Cows were grazing where the yard used to be, and I was glad that the area was still very rural. There wasn't much traffic, so I drove slowly by. I wasn't going more than ten miles an hour when I drove around the corner and saw that the Widow's house was still standing.

"The Widow" is what I called the woman who owned the large house when I was a little girl. She was my mother's best friend. I couldn't remember her real name.

I believe the Widow's only daughter was grown and gone before I was born, so I never met her. I was a late baby for my mother. My siblings were pretty much all in high school or middle school by the time I came along, so I was quite a bit younger than the Widow's daughter.

My mother liked to walk up to her friend's house. During the school year, she'd wait until my sister got off the bus to keep an eye on me, but in the summer, my sister worked. On a lot of hot, sticky afternoons, I would walk up the road holding my mother's hand. I have insect buzzing, green-tinted memories of those summer afternoon.

On hot days, the Widow would always give me a chocolate soda as soon as we got there and then she'd chase me out into the yard so she and my mother could visit. I think it was chocolate milk mixed with soda water, but I liked it. I'd drink the bubbly, watery chocolate while I scouted the unkempt grass in the Widow's front yard. If I sat very still and watched, I would see movement in the grass and maybe the tip of a feral cat's tail. To me, the prize would be a kitten that wasn't wild yet.

While I hunted, I was bitten up by those invisible insects called "chiggers" or "redbugs." Too small to see, they infested the long, weedy grass. There wasn't enough bug spray in the world to keep those bugs from finding the tender parts of my skin and leaving welts. The worst ones were on the elastic of my underwear and behind my knees. My mother would put Mercurochrome on the bites and warn me not to scratch. After the bites were scratched, the Mercurochrome stung like needles.

On really hot nights, my mother would make a cot for me on the screened-in porch. I'd lie there, sweating onto the sheets while the frogs sang and the lightning bugs twinkled on the edge of the yard. I tried to imagine how much the Mercurochrome was going to sting if I scratched. Finally, I couldn't stand it anymore and would dig my fingernails into the bumps. The feeling of satisfaction was deeply intense, but the itch would come right back, amplified.

And I never did catch one of the Widow's feral cat's kittens. I never even came close.

That afternoon, I drove slowly by the ruined old house while I remembered the chocolate soda and the bug bites. Or rather, I meant to drive slowly by.

The two-story house was on the verge of tumbling to the ground. The windows were dark holes, and kudzu-covered most of the rotten, gray wood on the right-hand side of the house. The thick, green vines looked like they were swallowing the house whole, but the bright red hatchback parked in the front yard was fairly new.

The car's hatch was open and I saw several flats of flowers, some of which had spilled over. I might have driven on, but there was a woman digging in the area on the left side of the house. A glance told me the woman was too old to be out in the heat, even if the house's shadow covered her. She had a shovel in her hands and seemed to be scraping at something.

This was none of my business. Old doesn't mean incapable, so I was afraid that I would insult her if I stopped to check on her. I had no idea who she was, or why someone would plant flowers in a weed-choked ruin. As I passed, I could see that she was bent with a dowager's hump and that she was old to the point of frail. She was trying to dig, but instead made frantic, choppy motions with the shovel.

In the middle of the road, I backed up and pulled into the yard, parking behind the hatchback. I sat for a minute in my car's air-conditioning and looked at the place while things I'd forgotten came to mind.

There used to be a flower bed where the old woman was digging. I remembered balancing on the stones, the chocolate soda in one hand while I kept an eye out for kittens in the grass. Once, I lost my balance and almost stepped on a black snake that was curled up in the marigolds.

I thought that maybe the digging woman was the Widow's daughter and wanted to plant flowers again. She was certainly old enough. Turns out, I was right. She was the Widow's grown-up-and-gone-away daughter, but she wasn't planting flowers.

It occurred to me that it was possible that the elderly woman remembered my family. And, even if she didn't, she should absolutely not be trying to dig in the heat, in the weeds, next to a house that was about to collapse.

The yard had to be infested with redbugs and ticks, not to mention the possibility of a snake or two. There were copperheads in the area when I was a kid. I had no bug spray in the car, and whatever the old woman was doing was none of my business, but I got out of the car anyway.

After the air-conditioning, it felt too hot to breathe.

The old driveway had sparse, knee-high grass. Still wearing my funeral suit minus the jacket, I picked my way around the red hatchback. It had bumper stickers under the open hatch. One proclaimed that the driver was "A Proud Parent of a Layton Hall Elementary Student" and the other spelled out "co-exist" with religious symbols. These told me that the very old woman probably wasn't the owner of the car. A gallon-sized azalea spilled out on the ground, and small squares of yellow and orange chrysanthemums had been knocked all over the inside of the car.

Even though this was none of my business, it was fishy enough to warrant calling the police, maybe on the non-emergency number.

Instead, I called out, "Hello, ma'am?"

I was retired and going gray, but the woman poking at the dirt with a shovel was at least old enough for me to call her "ma'am." She wore a polyester dress and compression stockings instead of gardening clothes. Her face looked red and mottled. She could barely pick up the shovel that she thumped to the ground, over and over.

The flower bed was long gone, but several stones still marked the area.

I didn't want to startle her. I called out, "Ma'am," as I circled around to come into her line of sight. God, I thought we were both going to be eaten alive by bugs.

Red-faced, she rested against the shovel and spoke with firmly to me. "You're trespassing. You got no business here, so get back in your car and go on."

"Yes, ma'am, I realize that, but I was just driving by my parents' old place. The Smith farm?"

The old woman squinted at me, so I told her, "My mother was Ida Lee Smith. She lived a mile down the road. By any chance do you remember her? I was passing by and saw you digging. I don't want to interrupt you, but I wondered if you're the Widow's daughter and if you knew my mother."

The old woman leaned on the shovel. She looked exhausted, but apparently, her eyesight was fine. She told me, "You're not one of Ida Lee's kids."

I explained. "I was the youngest. She had me when she was in her forties. If you're the Widow's daughter, then we probably never met."

The old woman nodded. "Well, I didn't know Ida Lee had another one. Yes, I knew your momma well. I suppose that she's passed away?"

My mother would have been over a hundred. "Yes, I'm afraid so."

"Sorry for your loss. You resemble the family, I can see that. You best go on. Your momma's house isn't there anymore." Her tone was softer, but she still wanted me to leave. I couldn't just leave her there, and there was nothing I could say that would be polite.

She waved her hand, shooing me away. I didn't move. We stared at each other for a moment until she shrugged. "If you're thinking you can't leave an old woman out here in the heat, then maybe you can help me with the digging since you're almost family. I could use a bit of rest."

I have to admit, I liked it when she called me "almost family."

There was nowhere for her to sit down, so I hurried back to the car to get the lawn chair from the trunk. I like estate auctions and the portable chair travels with me wherever I go.

Going back to the car gave me a minute to try to remember the family name of the Widow or her daughter, but it was no good. I had no idea what their names were.

I brought the chair back, hoping that she could comfortably sit in it. It was one of those canvas chairs that folded up, but it was a good one. "Here you go." I helped her get settled in the chair. God, I hope her compression stockings kept those damned bugs off her legs. My legs were starting to itch already, especially behind my knees. By the next day, we were both going to look like we had chicken pox.

She settled herself in the chair and studied the old ruin of a house. "I used to live here. Left when I was sixteen."

I felt like I was meeting a page out of my mother's history. "You're the Widow's daughter, right?"

She nodded. "Funny. I haven't thought of myself as anyone's daughter in a long, long time. But yes. My mother was a widow and your Ida Lee used to come visit. When I left home, Ida Lee only had four kids and the youngest was just starting school."

That meant she was probably at least twenty years older than my sixty-five years. That's way too old to be sweating in knee-high weeds. She hadn't offered me her name, nor had I offered her mine, so I kept calling her "ma'am." I asked her about the red hatchback, but she waved the question away.

Trying to be gentle, I pressed on. "My mother and I came up here, almost every day in the summertime. Lord, do I remember this place."

I looked at the old house. It used to be white with red trim, but even as a child, the paint was always flaking off. Some afternoons, I'd chip at the red paint on the door, even though my mother told me not to. I remember taking those bright chips of paint and sitting on the steps. I'd use them to make shapes of things like apples and cars.

The steps were gone and the house was a uniform rotten-wood gray. I remember that it was made of rough cut wooden planks. It was never a pretty place, but it was large and roomy compared to our house. It was cooler in the summer than our tiny little cottage, but drafty-cold in the winter. There was a fireplace in every room downstairs. I don't remember going upstairs, but I probably did.

The remains of the chimneys were smothered in vines. Though the dark windows, I could see weeds growing in the shadows and that let me know there wasn't very much flooring left. Most of the vines were kudzu, but I also spotted the heart shaped leaves and twisted flowers of morning glory. In the morning, that side of the house might look nice, in a ruined, blue-blooming sort of way.

My mother loved morning glory, even if she said it was a weed. She said that my father always threatened to tear it down if she let it get out of control.

Before I even realized I'd spoken, I asked, "What was my mother like?" My mother died when I was only twenty, and I'd never known her as an adult. She was always just my mom.

She looked at me with a firm expression on her face. "She was a good woman. Ida Lee killed my father, but she did it for me. And she helped bury him."

I think I said, "What?"

The Widow's daughter looked at me like she was irritated. "You asked a question and I answered it."

So I said, "But why would my mother kill your father?"

Smooth as anything, she answered, "Because of that baby. He's buried under there. I want him out of there before they bulldoze this house."

There was no way my mother killed some man and buried him in a flowerbed. I thought that it was time to dial nine-one-one and get the old lady back to the home. I assumed there'd be a Silver Alert out for her and maybe a bulletin out on a stolen red hatchback as well.

But I didn't do any of that. Instead, I wiped my sweating face on my sleeve and asked, "Why would my mother kill anyone and then bury him in the little flower bed? Why do you want your father back?"

She peered at me with deep eyes that were as bright as a child's. "I don't want my father back. Daddy's burning in hell and that's okay with me. He's buried over at the church, but I let Momma and Ida Lee put that baby in this flowerbed."

I listened because she kept talking, but I was trying to process the idea that she said my mother killed a man and that there was a baby buried in the flower bed.

The old woman shifted a little in the canvas chair and admitted that lately, she'd been worried about leaving the baby in the flowerbed. She said, "It was okay back then, but the property is going to be sold after I die." She asked me if I already knew any of this, but then she answered her own question. "I don't guess Ida Lee told anybody about that day."

Sitting there in the heat, watching the shadow of the house get longer, she said, "I don't care anymore who knows. I don't want them to tear this house down not knowing there's a baby buried right here. I don't want him scraped up like rubble and burned with the old wood, or carried to the landfill and left for trash. His skeleton has to be small, so they'll bulldoze right over it and not even know he's there."

I reached for my pocket to get my phone, but, of course, my jacket was in the car and my phone was in the pocket.

The old woman waved a fly away from her sweaty face. "Maybe I should stop talking now. Ida Lee wouldn't like it, me involving you in what happened. You go on and leave me to what I have to do."

Using the shovel like a crutch, she struggled to get out of the canvas chair.

I put my hand on her shoulder and held her down, but gently. Lord, there was nothing but sharp bone in that shoulder. I said, "Look, I'm not about to leave and you know it. You just blurted out something outrageous because you don't want me to leave. You want me to help you shovel that flowerbed up."

She settled back into the chair. "Well, either you'll dig, or you'll call the law, tell them what I said, and then they will dig him up. In any case, that baby is going to be out of that flower bed, so that's okay."

For a few minutes, we stared at each other. It didn't stop until a fly landed on her forehead and she waved it away.

Now, I know I should have called the authorities right then and there, but I didn't. I also didn't start digging, but I took the shovel and looked her in the eye. "I want the whole story."

She didn't seem to have a problem with that. In fact, she said, "You got a spine on you, just like Ida Lee. I don't suppose it will hurt anyone if I do tell you. This little soul in the flower bed was something I didn't want. I still don't, but I've come to think it wasn't right, what was going to happen to his remains when they knock this old place down."

The sun was low enough that the no-see-ums were coming out. I felt an almost-sting along my wrists. I flipped a tick off her arm. The skin felt thin and cool. I thought maybe that wasn't good. She should still be sweating.

"Was that a tick? Thanks. I hate them damned bugs. They used to get into my room. That was my bedroom up there. I was still a child, only fifteen, when I spent four months up there by myself. That's so no one would see me after I got big with the pregnancy. I remember that it was hot like it is now, and the bugs kept finding a way into my room that summer. I sewed a tear in the screen with black thread to keep the mosquitos and spiders out, but they found their way in anyway."

I didn't want her to stop talking, so I didn't interrupt, but I looked up at the window. It had no screen or glass left, but I could visualize a young woman sewing with black thread.

"Momma and Ida Lee were friends before, but it wasn't until I couldn't hide the baby growing in me that she and Momma became so close. Ida Lee had some nursing before she married, so Momma got her to help. I hated that baby inside me. It never stopped. I felt that baby kick, and it was like his seed was twisting around inside me. All those months, my momma crying and him...he kept saying "sorry, sorry" but there I was in that room, sewing until that screen looked like a big, black veil."

She looked at the upstairs windows. There were no boards left on the one in the middle window. There was nothing but a dark hole. I asked, "That room?"

"Up there, I even stabbed my belly with a pair of scissors, but it only scratched my skin. I didn't want to die, but I wanted that thing inside me to go away. Your Ida Lee checked on me and when my time came, she delivered my baby. I barely cried out. It was okay to feel that pain because I was pushing the last of him out of me."

I believe I whispered to tell her how sorry I was, but perhaps I only thought it. I didn't want to stop her talking.

"The baby finally came out of me and it felt like my father was finally out of me at the same time."

I knew what was coming, but it still made me want to cry out when she said that it was her own father.

She had her eyes tightly shut. "Once the baby was out, I was so relieved that I almost didn't hear Ida Lee say that the baby was a boy and that he wasn't right. I only looked quick. All I saw was this little red fist waving around and all of a sudden, it opened up as if the baby had startled. There were four little fingers and a thumb and it looked perfect. He cried out, but it was a thin sound and I looked away."

I kept looking at the dark window. It was easier than looking at her. I noticed, for the first time, that the windowsill had the remains of an art-deco design.

She kept talking as I stared up at the window.

"Momma took the baby while Ida Lee finished up with me. He was wrapped in a white towel. Momma tried to get me to hold the baby, but I wouldn't even look. I didn't want it. I didn't want to see its perfect hand and I didn't want to see what was wrong with him. Another cramp hit me and while Ida Lee delivered the afterbirth, my daddy knocked on the door. My momma screamed at him to leave me alone, just leave me alone. She yelled that it was his fault, and she wasn't going to pretend he didn't do what he did. I remember her screaming at that closed door, holding the baby in that towel. She had her hand over the baby's head like she was covering his ears. Real calm, Ida Lee finished what she was doing with me, got up and told Momma to move her hand. She said not to put her hand on the baby's face."

I looked back at the old woman. All the pain from decades earlier was still there.

"I was fifteen. Fifteen. And I still I don't know if Momma smothered that baby or if he died naturally."

She pulled a tissue out of her pocket and wiped her face. "My daddy banged on the door one more time and said that he was sorry, that he hadn't meant for this. He was sorry like he'd been saying for months. Ida Lee went to the door and opened it a little bit. She had a little blood on her hands, but she held that door so he couldn't see in. Ida Lee told him that it was important that he leave me alone right then. Her voice was soft but angry. I remember how red-hot angry it was inside each little word.

"Daddy asked about the baby, and I remember so clear, how Ida Lee's hand left a smear on the door. She told him that the baby was a boy, but that he wasn't right and wouldn't live."

"Daddy said something about fixing the fence at the pasture, and for Ida Lee to tell him when it was time to dig the hole. Your momma shut the door in his face."

The Widow's daughter was in pain, telling that story. She turned slightly and looked to an overgrown area behind the house. "After he left, Ida Lee took the baby from Momma. I don't think he was moving anymore. He wasn't crying. You're crying."

I nodded and wiped my face on my shirt sleeve.

The old woman's face didn't look too wet anymore, and I wondered if she was becoming dehydrated. She kept talking, though. "After she got me cleaned up, your mother told Momma to stay with me. Ida Lee took the baby and went downstairs. Momma tried to comfort me, but I wouldn't let her. She never stopped Daddy, even when it was just tickling me or touching too much. I never believed she didn't know. As far as I was concerned, I'd just pushed the last of him out of me and I was never going to let anyone touch me again and that included her."

All I could think to say was, "No. I guess not."

She tucked her tissue back into her pocket and kept talking. "Ida Lee took the baby downstairs, and I know she put him in an empty ammunition box that Momma kept her sewing in. It had a hinged top, which made it like a little chest. She left the baby and the box on the front porch when she went and followed my daddy out to the cow pasture."

The Widow's daughter sat in my canvas chair and told me what happened. She said, "A little while later, Ida Lee came back to the house, came upstairs, and she admitted it right out. I was in my bed, hurting and bleeding a little, and sweating. God, sweat was pouring off me, and Momma kept trying to mop my face, but I wouldn't let her. Then here comes Ida Lee with blood splattered up her dress. Said Daddy was bending down to check a fence post and that he was crying. Said she picked up the hammer and that he didn't even put his hand up when she swung it and brought it down on him. We were upstairs, right there…."

The old woman pointed a bent finger at the empty windowsill. "And Ida Lee stood tall and still when she asked my Momma if she wanted her to go for the sheriff. Momma shook her head."

Hearing of how my mother clubbed a man to death made pride swell up in me. I didn't have time to think about whether it was right or wrong to feel what I was feeling. Crowded into my thoughts was worry about the traumatized, fifteen-year-old girl.

I blurted out, "Did they talk right in front of you? While you were in bed?" It was an odd thing to focus on, but I wanted to know.

She nodded. "Yes. I was glad they were talking in front of me. Ida Lee said I shouldn't do any stairs so I couldn't come downstairs to where they were going to bury the baby, but if I needed anything to call out. I did get out of bed, but only came over to the window even though it hurt to walk and it made blood run down my legs. I couldn't see them, but I heard them digging and I heard them praying over the dead baby. I pressed my face against the screen and listened to their praying words before they covered him up with dirt. It's strange, but I was sweating so when I pulled away from the screen, I felt the little pieces of black mending thread sticking to my face. I can still feel that." She actually wiped at her cheek, as if threads were still sticking to her.

I could picture the teenaged girl, her face pressed against the mended screen, watching us. "What did they do about your father's body?"

"After they buried the baby, Ida Lee and Momma went and rubbed some of his blood on the bull's back leg. That bull was as tame as they come, but the people in town didn't know that. Momma walked into town to get help, and Ida Lee said she found the body and tried to help him, so that's why she had blood on her."

I wondered if they believed her or just pretended to. Did the authorities in town know why the daughter was up in her room, with pieces of black thread caught to the sweat on her cheek?

The sunlight changed and the wind picked up. The fly that was annoying us disappeared. The old woman turned her face towards the breeze. "I didn't go to Daddy's funeral. People thought I was still recovering from some vague malady. That's what they used to say of girls who got pregnant and dropped out of sight for a while. They had a malady."

Abruptly, her face contorted with anger. She said, "My daddy had a real nice funeral. Lots of people came to pray over him."

I had no words in my head. I was deeply, deeply proud of my mother, but at the same time, I wondered if she attended the man's funeral. Of course, she did. Ms. Ida Lee Smith stood tall while she helped her best friend bury that man.

God bless that old woman for telling me this story. I am proud to be Ida Lee's child, even if she did commit a crime. But instead of thanking her, I found myself telling her how sorry I was about it all, but she waved it away.

"Storm's coming up, to the southwest. See those clouds? I never did have any more children, never married. As soon as I had enough age, I left to become a nurse too. Went into the Army and had a good life for myself. There's no one left to care about what my daddy did."

I told her that I cared. Very much. This place was where I grew up. This place is where I found out about my mother.

The poor old thing was worn out, but she just looked at the flowerbed. "I always felt bad about putting that baby in the dirt like that. It wasn't his fault that I didn't want him. It wasn't his fault at all, and he should be in the church's cemetery. He should have had a nice funeral, not my father. This had been on my mind.

"This morning, I was doing my morning walk around the parking lot at the home. That woman who plants things left her car running while she went and signed in. I guess she was going to drive around back where there's a little garden. I saw that car with a shovel in it, and I didn't even think about it. I was in the military and drove everything so that little red car was easy. It didn't even have a clutch, but once I got here, it took me forever to figure out how to open up the car's back to get to the shovel."

I asked her how she knew the house was still standing.

She said, "I still own this property, so I knew nobody tore the house down. The idea of someone finding the baby is okay. I don't mind him being found. There's no one left to get in trouble from him being in the flower bed but me, and who's going to come after a woman my age? No, what bothers me is the not-finding, having his remains bulldozed. And this old place is going to fall over soon, all by itself."

She shifted in the canvas chair. I knew it was probably cutting off the circulation to her legs, but she started speaking again, so I didn't interrupt her.

"I spent my life somewhere else, but when it was time for me to go into the home, I didn't feel connected to any person or any place."

God, I understood.

"I came back to the old folk's home that's only a couple of miles from here. All my friends died or wandered off and I felt lonely, so I came back here to try to come home. It didn't work. There was nothing here, except this rotting house with the baby buried in it. And I never told a soul about the baby."

"You just told me."

"Yes, but I wanted something from you. I still do."

All I could do was ask, "What were you planning to do with the baby once you dug him up?"

"I wasn't planning anything, really, except to get him out of the ground. Maybe we could get him reburied in a real grave, but I don't want him next to my parents at the church."

She leaned over in her chair as if she was going to touch one of the scattered rocks. I started to put my hand out because the canvas chair wasn't that steady, but she waved me away and straightened back in the chair. "Your mother helped. She helped more than I can say. Are you going to help me now?"

The shovel was in my hand and I didn't think about it. I should have called someone, but I didn't. I dug where she'd been scraping the dirt.

She told me, "You're in the right spot. Keep going."

I did.

The shovel hit wood only about six inches down. Most of the area's dirt is clay, but the old flowerbed had enough topsoil in it to be easy to dig. I used the shovel to free up the box, but when I got on my hands and knees and tried to pull it out of the dirt, only the disintegrating top came off.

The old wooden box was rotten, but it had done its job. It protected the baby.

Inside there was a brown, mottled rag that was sprinkled over with dead bugs and dirt.

"Can you pull him out of there?" The old woman leaned over in the canvas chair.

I shook my head as I folded back a bit of the cloth that fell apart as soon as I touched it. "It won't hold together if I try to pick it up. Wait..."

The cloth that tore away revealed part of a tiny skull. I couldn't even see how much of the skull was still intact and I didn't want to disturb the bunting anymore. "I can't pick him up without it falling apart, but can you see? He's here. Can you see him?"

She didn't look. Lightning lit up the sky. The clap of thunder wasn't that far away.

I ran back to the car and got the jacket I'd worn to the funeral off the passenger seat. When I pulled my jacket off the seat, my phone fell out into the grass, but I didn't stop to pick it up. I brought the jacket back to the grave and spread it on the ground. Using both hands, I scooped up the baby's remains. A lot of the blanket stuck to the box, but I had most of it in the first try. I laid the bundle on my jacket and added a few things that were still in the coffin-box. I was surprised that I didn't mind touching all the pieces. It even felt right to handle the loose dirt in the bottom of the disintegrated box. When I had all the pieces that counted, I wrapped the whole bundle up with my jacket and used the sleeves to secure it. Finally, I offered the sad little bunting to her.

She shook her head. "I'm sorry. I'm so sorry, but I still can't."

I sat on the ground and cradled the jacket-wrapped baby with one hand. With the other, I pulled up part of the box out of the ground. Under the piece that came out, I saw a rusted metal object. It wasn't hard to figure out that it was the hammer. Rather than try to remove the old murder weapon, I covered it back up. I was going to have to report this to someone, so I figured that I might as well leave the hammer alone.

Her voice was soft when she asked, "anyway I can convince you to get in your car and go? Take the baby, but leave me here?"

I said, "No." The wind picked up with the dark clouds that were rolling in. Otherwise, I think we might have just sat there. The storm was coming, and I had to get them both somewhere safe.

I helped her to my car and got her settled into the front passenger seat. I closed the hatch on the red car so the rain wouldn't damage it, but left my canvas chair. The wind knocked it over against the house anyway. Honestly, I forgot about my phone still on the ground somewhere. I didn't have time to worry about the shovel or the spilled flowers.

Bundled up in my jacket, I put the baby on the floor of the backseat. I didn't want to slam on my brakes and have the poor little thing fly off the seat.

The rain held off just a few minutes more, but the air pressed down as I slid into the driver's seat and slammed the door. Lightning lit up the house, in dark relief.

For a fraction of a second, I thought I saw threads of black in the window.

I blinked into the light. For several moments, I watched as the light bounced in my vision. I assume the Widow's daughter was blinking as well.

Just before the rain pounded, she said, "I want you to be Ida Lee's child right now. I want you to do whatever is right."

The rain started as I started the car. We sat in silence for a few minutes while the deluge drummed on the roof of the car.

I knew the authorities would have to be notified and there'd be an investigation, but evidentially they'd release the baby's body, especially after they'd heard the whole story. "With your permission, I'll bury him next to my mother. What name do you want on his tombstone?"

Because of the rain, I almost didn't hear her. "I think of him as my Henry. How could I name something I hated?"

As we stared through the windshield, I took her hand in mine, and for a moment, she squeezed my fingers. We stared at the old house as if it was going to fall under the weight of the storm. The rain had lightened up before she spoke again. "Put the name Henry Ida Lee Smith on that tombstone."

"That's a good name. I will," I promised.

About The Author

In the late fifties and early sixties, Rebecca Leanda grew up on both the eastern and western hemispheres. She often lived in areas that did not have niceties like televisions, but they always had books. Her first book memory was sitting cross-legged on the wrap-around porch of her tropical home, reading a "Little House On The Prairie" novel and feeling the coolness of the blue and white tiles on her legs while Laura Ingalls Wilder described living in a covered wagon.

She also vividly remembers the moment when she sat cross-legged in her grandmother's small living room. It was summer in Texas, and the rotating fan made a lot of noise, but she didn't mind because she saw the flickering image of a "Leave It To Beaver" re-run on a black-and-white television. Someone pointed out that a person wrote the lines for the actors to say, just like a person wrote books.
A real person wrote the stories.

It was a moment that would eventually come back and change her life.

Rebecca spent the first part of her adulthood in the Virginia suburbs of the D.C. area. Almost two decades ago, she moved to North Carolina. In between, she raised her four beautiful children, and moved from suburbs to the woods to the country. Her latest move took her to a home that is close to where her partner grew up.

She has a slight, southern accent, grows tomatoes and other country-type things, but still can't quite figure out some regional traditions like tomato sandwiches and Brunswick stew. Still, she's people-observant and is figuring out what life is like for people who grew up in one place.

And she became one of those people who write stories.

Rural Ruin

Simon Easton

Beer me," said Jacob.

Ren unhooked a beer from the first six-pack. He handed it to his friend who sat next to him on the dilapidated couch in the dilapidated house.

"It's kind of warm," Jacob complained.

"I told you we should have brought a cooler."

"How the hell are we supposed to get a cooler in here?" asked Jacob, sounding vexed. "It was hard enough just to get ourselves in here." Ren didn't agree with a lot of what Jacob said lately, but he had to admit to himself that a cooler would have been a pain in the ass, given how far they had to walk through the woods to get to the deserted house. But warm beer was a pain in the ass too.

"Give me another beer too," Pam said, tossing her empty can onto a pile of cans in the corner. It looked like a beer can snowdrift and it smelled of re-fermenting yeast and hops which mixed, not unpleasantly, with the smell of mildew and wood rot of the decomposing house.

Ren had to lean over to put the beer in her hand, as she was sitting on the far side of Jacob on the couch. She and Jacob had been holding hands before, but they weren't at the moment. Ren knew that because she took the beer with her left hand and not her right.

"We could have at least brought a bucket of ice," Ren continued.

"Oh, shut the fuck up, will you?" asked Jacob languidly.

Yellow streaks of sunlight played on the spray paint graffiti on the far wall of the room opposite to the broken window. It was not their graffiti. They weren't the only ones who had ever used the house, and they had to be careful not to sit on dirty needles or broken glass.

It would be dark soon. Ren had a Coleman lamp to light up the room when it got dark, but he was reluctant to turn it on. He did not want to be able to see them if they started holding hands again, or worse.

Ren wasn't a bad-looking guy, but he'd never had a girlfriend before. That was because his lifelong friend Jacob was exceptionally good-looking, and he had an easy sort of charm when it came to girls, and when Ren stood near him he tended to fade into the background. No one wants to date the friend of the hero. He didn't like being a third wheel, but he liked being alone and sober even less, so over and over he had told himself that he could continue to endure playing squire to Jacob's White Knight even though he hated it.

It still stung like a bitch, though. In fact, it burned.

Pam was pretty and dark and graceful in a way that tall girls usually aren't. She might have been an inch shorter than Jacob, but she didn't slouch or stoop or try to hide her height in any way. She was a goddess, and that made Jacob a god. Ren was the court jester who would always be in the shadow cast by the seemingly eternal union of Pam and Jacob.

The couple and Ren drank their beers and watched the sun crawl behind the horizon through the broken window.

"Someday this place is going to come down on our heads," Ren said as the house creaked against the cool autumn wind.

"We'll be too drunk to notice," Jacob said. "What we don't notice can't hurt us."

Ren watched the sky as it turned purple with the sunset. He could sense that Jacob and Pam were kissing, so he clenched his jaw and kept his eyes on the window until the sounds let up. He finished his beer, crushed the empty can, and threw it in the corner. He immediately opened another one, determined to have more than his fair share of the two six-packs they had snuck into the derelict house, determined to get spectacularly drunk to the point where everything is good and fine for the fifteen blissful minutes before the puking begins.

"I have to take a piss," Jacob announced.

"Good for you," Ren said. Pam laughed.

Taking a piss involved meandering around in the dark house to the back porch, avoiding the holes in the floor, and pissing off the top step into the woods. For a girl it was roughly the same, only she squatted on the front step with her ass to the woods instead of aiming for the nearest tree.

"Are you gay?" Pam whispered to Ren as Jacob made his way to the back of the house.

"What?"

"It's okay if you are," Pam said. "I won't tell Jake. It'll be like our little secret."

"I'm not gay," Ren said. He chugged his beer angrily, threw the empty can away, and popped another.

"How come I never see you with a girl?" Pam asked, her voice still pitched low.

"Jacob gets the girls," Ren said. "I'm just around for contrast. And to drink beer with."

"Maybe you're gay and you just don't know it."

"Maybe you're a cunt and you don't know it."

The creaky floorboards announced Jacob's imminent return. They both grew quiet. Ren got up for the fight that would begin when Pam told her boyfriend that Ren had called her a cunt. She didn't say anything, though. Jacob sat back down, but Ren remained standing, surprised that he and Jacob were not already bashing each other in the face.

Or maybe it would go another way.

"Beer me," Jacob said as he plopped himself back down on the couch with Pam. Ren reached down and twisted another beer off of the six pack and handed it over. It felt cooler now that he was hot with anger. "What did you two do while I was gone?" Jacob joked.

"Your girlfriend asked me if I was gay, and then I called her a cunt," Ren said.

"What?"

"You heard me."

"You're kidding, right?"

"No."

"It's a joke, right, Pam? It's a joke?"

"No," she said slowly.

"Jesus, Ren," said Jacob. "Now I have to beat the shit out of you."

"You don't have to do anything," Pam said firmly, tugging at his sweater as he rose. "Sit down." Jacob pushed her arm away.

"No," said Ren. "He's got to do this. It's the only thing he knows to do."

Jacob rose, and he and Ren began to slowly circle each other. Jacob chose his moment and flung himself at Ren. Ren stepped aside and planted his switchblade into Jacob's kidney as Jacob fell to the floor.

Ren had not decided to do it, but he hadn't decided not to do it either. It just happened that way.

The knifed boy tried to reach around his back to remove the blade.

"Don't," Ren said. "You'll just die faster."

"Oh my God!" Pam said. Her cell phone was out in a flash. Ren stepped over Jacob to smack the mobile out of her hands. It clattered across the room and against the wall, the shattered screen glowing in the darkened room. Then it went to sleep, and the room returned to what it had been a moment earlier.

"What the fuck is wrong with you?" Pam shouted. "Let me call a fucking ambulance!"

"No," said Ren. "I don't think so."

Pam screamed for help. Ren laughed.

"We're in the middle of nowhere. No one can hear you."

Pam started to get to her feet.

Ren punched her in the face. Some of the blood on his hand stained her cheek. "Sit down," Ren barked. "Unless you want some more." Pam obeyed. She began sobbing, her breath hitching in the way children cry when they are in deep trouble.

"I'm going to kill you," Jacob said through his teeth. "You little fuck."

"No, you're not." Ren grabbed a beer and sat himself in the doorway of the room's only exit. He drank deeply, grateful that no one could see his hands shaking in the gloom. "You're going to lie there and bleed to death. Then I'm going to take the knife out of your back and stick your girlfriend and watch her bleed to death."

"You won't get away with it," Jacob said.

"Really? Did you really just say that? Does this look like a fucking comic book to you?" Ren reached out with his leg and kicked him in the gut. Jacob cried out in pain. "I don't plan on getting away with it."

"Let me go get help," Pam begged. "You can leave. I won't tell them you did it. Just let me get help for Jake. Please."

"Fucking bitch. Didn't you hear what I just said?"

"Please, Ren. I'm sorry I asked you if you were gay. Just... please."

Ren finished his beer, threw the can into the corner, and popped another open.

"You think that's what this is about?" Ren asked.

"What else?" Pam asked back.

"If you knew what this shithead was really like, you'd know what else." Ren considered what he had just said. "But you like it, don't you? You like the way he rubs off on you."

"What are you talking about?"

"You're not people. You're both…accessories that look like people."

The alcohol was really beginning to hit Ren. He had to speak carefully so Pam would not hear him slur. She might get the idea that she could get past him. She might begin to think she was going to get out of this alive.

No one was getting out alive. At least, that was the plan.

Ren turned on the Coleman lamp. There wasn't as much blood coming out of Jacob as Ren thought there should be, and he was happy with that because Jacob would suffer longer. When he bent over Jacob to see how much blood there actually was, the wounded boy struck. He grabbed Ren by the hair and pulled him to the floor. Still holding onto Ren's hair, he punched Ren in the face more than once. The blows hurt, but they weren't crippling. Jacob was already too weak.

Ren untangled himself from the grip Jacob had on his hair by prying his fingers back until they loosened enough for him to pull his head away. Some of his hair had come out by the roots and it hurt like hell. Ren kicked Jacob in the gut a few more times to teach him a lesson and then slid back out of Jacob's reach. He fully intended to knife Jacob again, but he would have to wait until Jacob had grown weaker to retrieve the weapon.

"What do you want?" Pam asked. "Why are you doing this?"

"I want the world to be fair," Ren answered.

"What?"

"I want life to be fair," Ren explained.

"How does killing us make life fair?"

"It evens things up. You're both so pretty and handsome and popular. You think you earned it, but you just got lucky. Now you've got to pay the price for your luck."

"What are you talking about?"

"I knew you wouldn't get it."

"Please! You've got to let me help him!"

"You should be more worried about yourself."

Pam started to cry again.

"Shut up!" Ren yelled. He got up out of the doorway to stand above her. "Just shut the fuck up!"

The crying didn't let up, so Ren smacked her in the head as hard as he could. She slid down across the couch and stayed there, silent.

"Asshole," Jacob spat, his voice inflected by his pain.

"Are you fucking stupid?" Ren asked. "I'm in charge here. You need to respect me."

"Bullshit," Jake said through his teeth. "You're still an asshole. You'll always be an asshole."

Ren turned on the Coleman light. He circled around Jacob, staying out of reach. Then in a swift motion he bent down and pulled the knife out of Jacob's kidney. Jacob screamed. He tried to stab Jacob in the back again, but the knife wouldn't go in far enough. He must have hit a rib. Jacob reached for him, but Ren skittered out of the way. He almost fell because of the slick puddle of blood surrounding Jacob, invisible despite the soft glow of the lantern.

By the time Ren was done with Jacob, Pam was semi-conscious. She managed to push herself up into sitting position. Ren crossed the room and twined her hair around his left hand.

"Did you know that Jakie brags about your body all the time?"

Pam shook her head no.

"He says you have really great tits," Ren said. He turned toward Jacob.

"Are her tits as nice as you say they are, Jakie?" Ren asked. "Let's find out." He used the knife to cut the buttons off her blouse. He was awkward with the tool because he was using it one-handed, and he ended up nicking her with the razor-sharp knife more than once. She gave off a little scream every time he cut her, and every time she screamed Ren told her to shut up.

Her blouse eventually came away from her bosom, revealing a surprisingly practical bra, like the ones in the Women's Department at Sears. Ren had always imagined something a little more Victoria's Secret, but it didn't really matter. Tits were tits. He cut the bra open between the cups and it dropped away to reveal Pam's breasts. Their pale white skin made them the brightest things in the dusky room.

Pocketing his bloody knife, he put his hands over her breasts and firmly squeezed each one. He flicked his thumbs over her areolas and erect nipples. Then he took his knife and flicked it open and closed and open again. He ran the flat of the blade over one breast and then the other. He could feel her tremble. He had a tremendous boner, and he had to concentrate so he wouldn't come in his pants.

"These are the best tits I've ever felt," Ren said. "You weren't kidding, were you, Jakie? Maybe I'll take one home with me."

"Please," Jacob said, his voice barely a whisper. "Please. I'm sorry."

"What are you sorry about, Jakie?"

"Calling you an asshole. Whatever I did."

"You really don't get it, do you?"

"You don't have to do this. There's still time."

Ren considered Jacob's words briefly and then rendered his verdict.

"It's too late for that," he said. "Too late for you and too late for me."

"It's not too late for…" Jacob hissed. Then he went silent. Ren could feel his lack of movement. His utter stillness. He knew that his friend was dead.

"Your turn," Ren said, turning toward Pam. She had drawn her shirt closed and had crossed her arms over her breasts defensively. Ren flicked the blade up and down over and over again.

"Fuck you," Pam said.

"What?"

"Fuck you," Pam repeated.

"What is it with you two? I have the knife," Ren said, confused. "Don't you think you should be nicer to me?"

"Why?" Pam asked. "Because you're a pathetic little shit who had to kill his best friend to get to second base? Fuck you."

Ren put the knife to her throat.

"What do you think now, cunt?"

He could feel her quivering through the blade.

"What are you waiting for?" Pam asked, her voice steady despite her trembling. "To grow a pair? It takes a big man to kill a girl."

Ren pressed the tip of the knife into her neck, just a little. Pam drew in a sharp breath through her teeth but she did not cry out. She closed her eyes.

"Holy shit!" someone said from the doorway. Ren jerked his head around to see who had spoken. He was a ragged man, a wino Ren knew no one would miss. As Ren moved the knife from Pam's throat and turned to kill the interloper, she punched Ren in the crotch with everything she had. He stood stock still for a moment, unable to move.

Then the pain kicked in. He dropped his knife, fell to the floor, and clutched himself. Something had to be busted inside him. It hurt that much. He rolled back and forth, moaning.

Pam picked up the knife and straddled him, her breasts swinging free once more. She raised the knife. Ren's arms were pinned under her legs and he could not get them loose.

"Hey, wait a minute, girl! Think about it!" said the man in the doorway. She raised the knife and paused for a second. Then she plunged the knife into Ren's chest and pulled it out slowly. There was a lot of blood, and it only took a few moments for Ren to start coughing it up.

"Did he do this?" the man asked, gesturing toward Jacob's body.

"Yes."

The more Ren tried to breathe, the more blood came up into his throat. He was drowning. The room began to drop away.

The man took a drink from his bottle sheathed in a paper bag and offered it to Pam. She took a drink, cringed, and gave him the bottle back.

"Then he deserves it," said the man.

"Feel free to have a beer," she said. "In fact, you can have the rest." The man immediately took one, popped it open, and drank deeply.

Pam looked down on Ren.

"Is it fair now?" she asked him.

He wanted to answer her, but his world was plunged into white-hot light instead.

About The Author

Originally from Pittsburgh, Pennsylvania, Simon moved to North Carolina in 1998 and taught in a low-wealth county for fifteen years. During that time, he taught middle school Language Arts to seventh graders and elementary school subjects to fourth and fifth-grade students. He continues to live in the county in which he was an educator.

When Simon isn't writing, he is keeping house, raising a son, or volunteering as a Guardian ad Litem.

The House On Guess Road

Dawn R. Taylor

1802
New Orleans, Louisiana

I came into being in 1802. I do not have a memory of existing before I transitioned into what I am now. I am a house. My roots are planted in the cool red clay dirt of Durham, North Carolina. Although I have not always been here, this is where I will cease to be because I have no desire to exist anyplace else. As a matter of fact, I have moved three times since becoming a house. Each move was harder than the one before it. Along the way, with each move, I have lost bits and pieces of myself, and that is never easy. I am two hundred and twelve years old and surprised that I am still standing.

I began my awareness in New Orleans, on the Rousseau plantation. My first memory of Monsieur Rousseau was of him yelling at the painters.

"More! I want more paint on de house. Check de couleur, I ordered sage and dis is not sage. What is wrong with you people! I could have gotten one of my feeble-minded slaves to do it better, and for nothing! I will not pay for des mauvais travail, imbéciles!" he said as he stormed off.

It took them two months to cover my cedar and complete their work. When they finished, I was a beautiful two story plantation home. I knew I was beautiful because of the way Monsieur Rousseau stood back and smiled when he first saw me completed. He didn't take a breath the whole time he stared at me.

My soul was born at that moment. A divinely fearless magnificent soul.

Other than the main house to my left, there wasn't another house for miles that could dwarf my beauty. Live oaks lined both sides of the pathway that led to my front porch. The porch had four tall round pillars. Large weaved fan back chairs and finely crafted tables decorated it. I was a serene sage with linen-colored shutters and doors eagerly awaiting visitors. Inside the front door was a modest foyer adorned with family pictures. To the left of the foyer was the large living room and kitchen, and to the right of the foyer was a library with a small office in the back. My stairs led up to a large hallway and three bedroom suites. All my walls were white except the kitchen which was a pale yellow.

I waited and longed for someone to live in me and to love in me, for someone to make beautiful memories in me so that I might grow and flourish. You see, I need these energies to feed my spirit and to make a house into a home. It's not good for a home to be alone.

In 1806, my dreams of becoming a home came true when Monsieur Rousseau brought his sister-in-law to live in me, and I was thrilled. Mademoiselle Élisabeth Matoivé was a beautiful little thing, not more than five feet tall and a hundred pounds. She was a loving spirit. Her hair was a dark wavy brown that she wore in an elaborate design with curls at the top of her head. Her large almond-shaped clear green eyes and olive complexion made men stare at her in a way that often made her look away and blush. Mademoiselle Élisabeth was to be married in May and moved to New Orleans to finish her education before the marriage. Her English was not very good, but she had a tutor and spoke English with French breaks in it.

She was fifteen years old and naive when she came to me. I wondered why she had a house of her own at such a young age, but I learned that Madame Rousseau didn't want her beautiful young sister living in the main house with her and her husband. I didn't understand because Mademoiselle was such a lovely being. I enjoyed watching her as she learned proper English with her tutor, replacing French words with the correct English ones.

Many days she wrote poetry that she read aloud to herself and I pretended she was speaking to me. I watched her dance around and sing like an angel to no one in particular. She spent most of her time alone and I often feared she would go mad. I learned that it is not good for humans to be alone. She was not allowed off the property without a chaperone and it seemed no one wanted to be responsible for her. The few times that Madame Rousseau did visit her sister she would reduce Mademoiselle to tears with spiteful words.

The first time Mademoiselle cried because of her sister's venom, I felt my wood floor in the root cellar crack. Occasionally, Monsieur Rousseau stopped by to fix things around the house and he watched her without her knowing. I could see, though, how he watched her. His intentions swirled around him like a swarm of bees. When I saw him in the distance, headed my way, I would swell my wood at the door making it difficult to open because his spirit was riddled with darkness. It didn't matter. He always managed to come in despite my best efforts. There were times when the Rousseau's managed goodwill toward Mademoiselle and allowed her to have dinner with them when they were not entertaining.

One sticky evening, the sky darkened and a storm lulled on the horizon. I knew there was more in the thunder than just noise. I checked on Mademoiselle and she was safely tucked in her bed singing to herself, trying to drown out the loud booms that came with each lighting strike. I listened to the beautiful sound as it escaped her lips and was almost sleep when something pushed against my front door. I looked down and saw Monsieur Rousseau creeping in quietly. His intentions were clear because the evil stuck to him like black tar and the smell of his thoughts was rancid. I shook the house enough to wake Mademoiselle and she sat straight up in the bed and called out.

"Who es there?" There was fear in her voice.

"It is just me Mademoiselle. I am closing des shutters."

"How kind of you, yes. Merci." She went back to her room.

I watched as she closed the door and laid down. It took all I had to swell the door jamb shut and I trembled as he sat at the table contemplating his next move. He tossed back three shots of bourbon and sweat poured off his large sticky body. His beefy protruding belly jutted under his nightshirt as he moved to the stairs. The thunder split the air with a magnificent boom and he was at her door.

I tried to keep her door closed, but he was determined. He entered, and with each violation I felt my wood begin to split, dull and curl. Mildew grew rapidly in those cracks that night. When he left, she was not the only one scarred and broken. That day was the beginning of my destruction. My front porch was weakened and splintered with every visit from him. The paint melted at the corners and four of my shutters fell off. The joy that once held me together was replaced with sour, foul odors that oozed from the cracks in my foundation. Black vines sprang from my dead wood.

It was March when he stopped coming and allowed her to get married and move away. She left, but she left behind all the sadness, distrust, fear, and pain. That was what was left here, here in me, here in this place. I sat empty, trying to remember the eagerness in which I prayed for someone to live and love in me, to bring me a wonderful life full of memories, but now I longed to be left alone.

1827

New Orleans, Louisiana

On August 22, 1826, Monsieur Rousseau was shot and killed by the brother of a young woman he had violated. He died right there on my magnificent lawn. His fetid blood seeped into my foundation.

Madam Rousseau died eight months later in childbirth. I do not know what happened to my beautiful Mademoiselle and this made me very sad. In 1862, war broke out and I was badly burned on my south side by a cannon hitting one of the oak trees. Unable to contain myself, I fell to the ground and was left in the field to rot away.

There I was, despondent and broken in the woods. I had sunk into a grief-fueled stupor when a young slave woman and her family used some of my bits to make a shelter. They were hiding from the men on horses. They stayed with me for two days and then they moved toward freedom, taking some of my smaller bits with them. It gave me joy, and I began to regenerate.

Over the years, others would find me and use my bits and pieces for their comfort.

Finally, in 1925, the salvageable parts of me were loaded on a truck and moved to Savannah, Georgia. I was put together again in 1926. They painted me a sky blue and my shutters a dark blue. I stood there in the cul-de-sac praying that this would be where my roots would form, new healthy, strong roots, fed by love, peace, and wonder. I prayed that the poison that had infected me in New Orleans was all gone.

1938

Savannah, Georgia

The smell of lemons woke me. The way Madeline, my new owner, used the soft cloth to rub my walls while she sang along with the radio made me feel safe. She was good to me and good for me. The day that she and her husband, Bruce, came to look at me, she named me. I was surprised and I blushed as she laid her cheek and hand against my body and whispered.

"Your name is Edrei because you are beautiful and strong. You will be the keeper of my secrets."

It was the most intimate moment of my existence. I warmed my wall beneath her cheek as I blushed. They made an offer on me that day.

The doorbell rang in the middle of Madeline's cleaning. I looked outside of myself and recognized the ladies standing at the door. They were trouble, all staunch, reserved and emanating self-righteousness. It promised to be interesting.

"Good morning Miss Madeline," the cheery voices sang out.

One woman continued, "We are here to welcome you to the neighborhood."

"Um, hello," Madeline said as she brushed her mousey brown hair out of her face.

"We are the Orchard Lake Community Welcoming Committee, and we are here to help y'all get acquainted with your new neighborhood and all it has to offer."

I got cold and creaked under the weight of their subterfuge. There was nothing welcoming about these creatures.

"Oh, how nice. Please excuse my appearance, but we were working on the house until late last night and I am not prepared for company."

"Of course. My name is Beatrice Walker and this is Vivian, Grace, Ruth, and Edith. We will be more than happy to come on back later. In the meantime, here is some nourishment to get your day started. I made the cherry pie and Vivian here, she made her famous cinnamon streusel muffins."

Madeline stood off to the side of the door and allowed the ladies access into me. The ladies filed into the box-filled foyer. Beatrice, without saying a word, walked into the kitchen and set down the pie on the counter. She returned to the group and told Vivian to hand the muffins to Mrs. Madeline.

"We won't take up any more of your time," Beatrice said. "We'll call on you again later in the week after you have had time to get your house in order. Please feel free to call me if you need anything as I live the closest. I have left an invitation to our annual Fourth of July shindig with my number on it next to the pie." With that said, Beatrice opened the door and walked out with the others following close behind. It reminded me of the mother duck and her ducklings crossing the pond behind me.

In the kitchen, I managed to sigh and knock the invitation into the trash where it belonged. Beatrice had a malignant spirit.

I was thrilled when Madeline closed the door and locked out any more interruptions. I waited for her to get the soft cloth and finish my massage. Instead, she exhaled as she walked into the kitchen and searched the icebox. She poured a glass of milk.

"You know, Edrei," she said, eyeing the muffin and picking at it, eating little bits at a time, "I know what those ladies were up to. Bruce says it's southern hospitality, but I say it was just nosiness." She giggled before taking a large bite. "Damn, that's good."

When Bruce came home from work, Madeline ran into greet him and asked,

"So are Lanie and Carl coming Friday?"

Lanie was her love in New York and Madeline missed her dearly.

"Can I get my jacket off first?" He took his jacket off in slow motion and hung it on the coat rack just inside the foyer. He walked into the kitchen, sniffed the air, and asked "What's for dinner?"

"Nothing. We are going out so the neighbors can see a loving couple. You know how these people like to see what is Biblically correct in the Bible Belt."

"Oh Madeline, I'm tired. Can we just eat here?"

"Fine, but all we have are pie, eggs, cheese, muffins, milk and bread," she said as she closed the icebox.

Madeline looked at Bruce and said, "So, are they coming?"

"Yes, I will pick them up after work."

Bruce changed his shoes and shirt. He picked up his jacket, turned to Madeline and said "Shall we?" They held hands as they walked to the car.

I am not sure when it happened, my understanding of my family. I think it came a few months later when Madeline was full of a rusty

melancholy. I realized that while these two loved each other, they were not in love with one another. From what I could gather, being who they were was dangerous and getting married was what they did to save their lives.

She laid across the couch and said, "I miss Lanie so much. I miss her touch, her kisses, and her body. I think I am in love. You don't understand how dangerous that is for me, Edrei. Love, love means making a decision I am not ready for. Love means throwing caution to the wind. I-I am not ready for wind."

I thought it was a good thing. Love is always a good thing, right? Love was the first bloom of a purple rose. It smelled of vanilla cream sprinkled with cinnamon and tasted like ecstasy. I was not sure how this could be bad. Whenever she talked about Lanie to Bruce, her aura became willowy pale yellow. So why was she melancholic and speaking of danger? Didn't she know I would never allow danger in? Never again would danger get in.

Madeline and Bruce sat across from each other at the dining room table. Madeline looked up and said. "Playing the dutiful wife is getting boring, Bruce. I miss the freedom that New York offered. We had our friends that knew who we really are. I don't understand why the promotion meant you had to come out here. You could have been a senior editor in the New York office." She put the broccoli stalk in her mouth. "I think someone found out about you and that's why we were banished all the way out here."

Bruce sighed. "I don't feel like having this conversation again."

"You are such a whore. I told you to be careful about who you were screwing, but no. You had to do as you please. I bet you screwed some important idiot's son." Her aura turned gray and bubbled.

Bruce crossed his legs and smirked, "Your claws are showing, dearie. I was not the only whore on Greenwich Street. I seem to remember your bedroom door revolved as quickly as mine."

"I want to go home." Her voice was weak when she said it.

He got up from his seat and came over and hugged her. "It's only been a little over a year. I have done the best I can by bringing Lanie out here at least once a month to see you, haven't I? Jason Fitz in the New York Office says that an opening is coming up in September as the head of sales, and he is putting my name in the mix." He squeezed her a little. "Just hold on. He kissed the top of her head, just hold on. I will get you back there."

"Okay," she said

I was crushed. I wanted to ask her what was wrong with me. Why didn't she want to stay with me? I loved her and Bruce. Most nights I watched over them when they slept. I kept them safe. I even scared away that old Beatrice hag when I caught her looking through the bedroom window in the middle of the night by dropping a piece of shingle on her that made her scurry away into the darkness. What more could I do? I finally had roots, and it felt so good and so right. The pain of rejection bent me. It took me a week to come out of my funk.

One evening Bruce came in the door, threw his jacket on the couch and said, "Let's go to the neighborhood barbecue," as he looked out the window at their neighbors.

"They have the whole cul-de-sac blocked off." He turned and looked at Madeline, who said no coldly. He shook his head in disgust and walked out the door.

Later that night the creaking noise woke me. Something was dragging along the floor and then it was clear. Madeline was sobbing. We cried together as that ugly man hit Bruce. His face was bloody and swollen. Bruce cried too. They drug him up and onto a chair at the end of the two twin beds. They tied his hands behind his back and covered his mouth with silver tape. My new roots died. Madeline was told to get up and sit in front of her husband. She shook in fear and I tilted a little to the east. My foundation trembled. Madeline smiled at her husband, confident and friendly. She mouthed the words "I love you" before the tall man with the white hood struck Bruce in the head with the butt of his rifle.

"Your husband is a sodomite and an abomination! He was fornicating with a man in the park. And like Sodom and Gomorrah, he will burn in Hell for his sin." They stood Bruce up, pulled down his pants, cut off his penis and cut his throat. His body dropped to the floor with a horrific thud. It happened so fast I shook to the east and then I shook to the west. I shook until my floor opened up and swallowed my Bruce. I used all I had to protect him from further desecration and had nothing left to help my beloved. And in that moment of my weakness they slit Madeline's throat. I stood silent and deaf. I blew out all the lights in the house. Inside and out. And then I moaned and wailed. Finally, someone called the police about my noise. Those hooded men wrote such horrible things about my family on my walls. I could not risk allowing that darkness to seep into me, but I didn't have enough strength and it was sucked into to me. I had no more strength or beauty.

I was no longer Edrei.

1980

Savannah, Georgia

I do not know what happened throughout the years after I lost my name, family, and will. There were many who moved in and out of me randomly, never loving me back to life. I do not know if it was them or me.

The years blurred into one another, never getting a spark out of me. I heard the noise of the crane and I didn't care. It was a warm night when they came. So many of them. They filled up the whole cul-de-sac. Each one was holding candles, swaying back and forth, and singing. One of them stood in front of the crowd and with a loud speaker. They read the names of other people like my Bruce and Madeline, who were killed. When I heard a girl actually say Bruce and Madeline Meyers, I was able to exhale the pain out of me. I vomited up all the leftover blood and devastation. I welcomed the wrecking ball as it hit my second story window. I embraced the destruction because out of the destruction would come another chance at utopia. They tore the rest of me down and laid me in pieces on my crumbled foundation. Some men came and decided my leftover parts could be useful and I was moved.

I was in a reuse and restoration store when the Framework for Families charity came and bought me, minus my more damaged parts. I was taken to Durham, North Carolina.

1990

Durham, North Carolina

I wasn't sure why they put me back together. My beautiful cedar had warped and had turned a dreary water-logged brown. I was not large or roomy. I was not fancy or painted. I had no pretty shutters or intricate details to boast of. And yet, there I stood in all my nakedness. I stood there at the end of Guess Road, in a field, across from the only store for miles.

My worries, wants, and needs had changed over the years. I no longer wanted a family or desired human contact. Humans, you see, are as unpredictable as nitroglycerin and twice as destructive. So I stood there and watched from afar the evil that men do. I watched the people as they came in and out of the store having loud, sometimes violent conversations. I watched as young lovers parked just outside my door and made love, laughed, cried and made promises they could not keep. I watched as things changed around me and ultimately stayed the same. I was content in the knowledge that this was how things would be...I was safe.

Then the giggling started. It was faint at first, but it grew until it could not be ignored. I was not sure where it was coming from, and, to tell you the truth, I was too weary to find out. Finally, able to, I searched for the origin of the noise. It came from inside of me, and yet I could not see what was making the noise. I had spent so many years looking outside of myself at others that I missed what was going on inside of me. I took self-inventory, and, there in the living room, I saw him. He was beautiful, and I held my breath. He could not have been any more than six years old and he was giggling. He was giggling, laughing and rolling around on the floor as a puppy licked his face. He was a joy and a savior. His aura was a supernova of innocence that would feed me until I was able to breath on my own. I was reborn.

About The Author

Dawn R. Taylor is a writer and abstract painter. Raised in Flatbush, a multicultural section of Brooklyn, NY her creative side was easily fed by all the different sights, smells and music that appeared in her neighborhood. At seventeen she joined the army, lured by the promise of travel to faraway places. While serving her country, she wrote poetry and short stories for her friends to enjoy. After she completed ten years of military service, she returned to NYC to attended the Borough of Manhattan Community College. While studying she read a book called Tally's Corner by Elliot Liebow that inspired her to write her first novel while sitting in front of a neighborhood deli on the corner of Hudson and Franklin St. She has since written countless short stories two other novels.

Dawn R. Taylor is currently writing and painting at her studio Artistically Speaking in downtown Durham North Carolina.

Works In Progress

Works in Progress is a group of dedicated writers in all stages of their literary and publishing careers. The group builds up its writers through critiques of works in various stages of development from inception to completion with a primary focus on short story critique, critiques of novels in progress, and critiques of full manuscripts.

www.ingramcontent.com/pod-product-compliance
Lightning Source LLC
Chambersburg PA
CBHW070803120626
46557CB00002B/695